DANNY'S LAST CHANCE

Jessica folded her arms across her chest. "Are you going to let me tell you the story or not?"

"Sorry. Go on," Elizabeth said.

"Well, Danny got called to the principal's office," her twin began. "And Mr. Clark told Danny that if he gets into trouble one more time, he's off the track team—for good."

Elizabeth couldn't believe it. Danny had never gotten into this much trouble before. "Maybe he'll be really careful from now on," she said. "He practically lives for track. There's no way he's going to let himself get kicked off the team."

"Want to bet?" Jessica asked. "When's the meet?"

"It's three weeks from yesterday," Elizabeth told her.

"Three weeks." Jessica shook her head. "Danny can't stay out of trouble three *hours*. He's not going to last three weeks without doing anything!" she predicted.

Elizabeth hoped she was wrong. Without Danny, the team couldn't possibly win!

Bantam Books in the SWEET VALLEY TWINS series
Ask your bookseller for the books you have missed

Sweet Valley Twins Super Editions:

Sweet Valley Twins Super Chiller Editions:

SWEET VALLEY TWINS

Danny Means Trouble

Written by
Jamie Suzanne

Created by
FRANCINE PASCAL

A BANTAM SKYLARK BOOK®
NEW YORK · TORONTO · LONDON · SYDNEY · AUCKLAND

RL 008-012

DANNY MEANS TROUBLE
A Bantam Skylark Book / August 1990

*Produced by Daniel Weiss Associates, Inc.
33 West 17th Street
New York, NY 10011*

Cover art by James Mathewuse.

ISBN 0-553-15806-6

Published simultaneously in the United States and Canada

---

*Bantam Books are published by Bantam Books, a division of Bantam
Doubleday Dell Publishing Group, Inc. Its trademark, consisting of the
words "Bantam Books" and the portrayal of a rooster, is Registered in
U.S. Patent and Trademark Office and in other countries. Marca
Registrada. Bantam Books, 666 Fifth Avenue, New York, New York 10103.*

PRINTED IN THE UNITED STATES OF AMERICA

OPM   0 9 8 7 6 5 4 3 2 1

One

◇

"Hi, Amy!" Elizabeth Wakefield called as she strolled up to the table where she and her friends Amy Sutton and Julie Porter usually ate lunch. Elizabeth sat down and pulled a sandwich out of her lunch bag.

"Where's Julie?" Amy asked.

"I haven't seen her since this morning," Elizabeth said. "She probably had to go to the library during lunch."

Suddenly there was a shriek from across the lunchroom. "Guess who," Amy said sarcastically.

"I don't have to guess," Elizabeth said calmly without even turning to look. "I'd recognize that sound anywhere. It's *got* to be Jessica."

"And her *herd* of friends," Amy added with a giggle. "A herd of purple Unicorns, that is."

Elizabeth and Jessica were identical twins. They had the same long blond hair, blue-green eyes the color of the Pacific Ocean, and skin tanned golden brown by the California sun. They looked so much alike that sometimes even their closest friends couldn't tell them apart.

But as identical as they looked, they had very different personalities. Elizabeth worked on *The Sweet Valley Sixers*, the sixth-grade class newspaper. She was very serious about her writing and hoped to be a journalist someday. She loved to read mystery novels and go horseback riding. And most importantly, she was a good friend.

Jessica didn't understand how Elizabeth could enjoy curling up with a book on a quiet afternoon when she could be hanging out at the mall instead. Jessica loved to spend time with her friends, listen to music, and shop for clothes. She was always keeping a close watch on the boys at school—especially certain ones in the seventh and eighth grades. Jessica was a member of the exclusive Unicorn Club, which only the prettiest and most popular girls in Sweet Valley Middle School were asked to join. Elizabeth thought most of the Unicorns were a little snobby, and at times she even referred to them as the Snob Squad. Elizabeth had an entirely different set of friends, most of whom Jessica thought were boring.

In spite of all of their differences, Elizabeth and Jessica were best friends. They had a special bond that only identical twins could have, and no one came close to knowing them as well as they knew each other.

Jessica jumped up from her seat, and headed straight for Elizabeth and Amy's table. ''Hi,

Elizabeth," she said as she came up to them. "Did you hear what happened to Julie?"

"We were just wondering where she is," Elizabeth said. "What happened?"

"Well," Jessica said, "you're absolutely not going to believe this!"

Elizabeth waited. Jessica had a flair for the dramatic, and even though she was acting like her news was earth-shattering, Elizabeth refused to get excited until she heard what it was.

"Tell us!" Amy demanded.

Jessica sat down at the table and began to relay her news. "Well," she said, "Danny Jackson was fooling around with a pair of scissors behind Julie's back in their science class this morning, pretending he was going to cut her hair. Everyone started laughing, and when Julie turned around to see what was going on—snip!" Jessica made a cutting motion with her fingers.

"You mean he *actually* cut her hair?" Amy asked.

Jessica nodded. "A huge hunk of it."

"What did Julie do?" Elizabeth wanted to know.

"She ran out of the room and hasn't been seen since," Jessica said. "She probably went home. That's what I would do. Then I'd stay home for two months until my hair grew back. I could watch *All the World* every day. That would be great."

"What did the teacher do?" Elizabeth asked. "Did he kick Danny out of class?"

"I don't think so. I think he just yelled at him," Jessica said.

"Danny's been getting into a lot of trouble lately," Amy commented.

"Yes, he has," Elizabeth agreed.

Danny had lived in Sweet Valley for only a few months, but he was already well-known at Sweet Valley Middle School. He was the best runner on the track team, *and* he was also the biggest troublemaker as far as his teachers were concerned.

"I wonder how many detentions he'll get this time," Amy said. "The teachers around here can be pretty strict."

"He should get at least a week's worth," Jessica declared. "If he did that to me, I'd be furious!"

"Me, too," Amy said. "I hope Julie's hair doesn't look terr—"

"Oh, great," Jessica interrupted her. "Look who's coming." She gestured toward the lunchroom door with her head. Caroline Pearce was heading toward their table. Caroline was the school's biggest gossip. She always had a story to tell. The only problem was that half the time, her stories weren't true.

"Hey you guys," Caroline said, "did you hear about Danny Jackson?"

Jessica sighed. "That's old news, Caroline," she said in a bored tone. "We know all about what he did to Julie's hair."

"Not that," Caroline said impatiently. "That

really *is* old news! I'm talking about what happened *after* that, when Danny was called to the principal's office."

"How do you know about that?" Elizabeth asked.

"Let's just say I have my sources," Caroline said smugly. "Anyway, I found out that he's not going to be able to run track anymore if he keeps getting into trouble like this."

"You're kidding!" Amy said.

"Nope." Caroline shook her head.

"But the team will never beat Pinecrest without him!" Elizabeth said.

"The meet's next Wednesday, isn't it?" Jessica asked.

Elizabeth nodded. "Pinecrest is one of the best teams in the area. The only way we can beat them is if Danny runs."

"It would be terrible if he got kicked off the team," Amy remarked.

"Well, I have to go," Caroline said. "See you later." Then she marched off to another table to repeat the news.

Elizabeth frowned. "This is pretty serious news about Danny."

"Maybe it's not true," Amy said hopefully. "After all, remember it was Caroline who told us about it."

Jessica flipped her silky blond hair over her shoulder. "Well, all I have to say is, if Danny comes near me with a pair of scissors, he'll be sorry!"

* * *

"Hurry up, Jess. We're going to be late," Elizabeth said the next Monday morning. The twins were getting ready to go to school, and as usual Jessica was behind schedule.

"Hold on a second!" Jessica called from her bedroom. "I just need to find something purple to wear." All of the Unicorns tried to wear something purple every day. It was their official club color because it was the color of royalty.

"I have a ribbon you could borrow," Elizabeth offered.

Jessica ran into her bedroom and Elizabeth handed the ribbon to her. "Just don't lose it, OK?" she said. She couldn't count the number of things she had loaned to Jessica and had never seen again.

"Oh, I won't. Don't worry," Jessica replied, tying the ribbon tightly around her ponytail. "I can't wait for school today! We've got an important Unicorn meeting. And I want to see what Julie's hair looks like."

"I told you, she went to the mall and got a trim on Saturday," Elizabeth said. She had called Julie over the weekend and gotten the whole story. Elizabeth was happy that Julie hadn't seemed too upset about what had happened.

"So how short is it? Does she have a crew cut or a mohawk or something?" Jessica asked.

"No." Elizabeth replied. "She just got it evened off."

"Oh." Jessica seemed disappointed that the

results weren't more drastic. "Well, are you ready to go, Lizzie?"

"I've been ready for the past fifteen minutes," Elizabeth said as she picked up her backpack.

"Then let's go!" Jessica said.

The warning bell was ringing as Jessica and Elizabeth hurried down the hall to their homeroom. A crowd was gathered outside the door.

"I wonder what's going on?" Elizabeth remarked.

"Maybe Mr. Davis is out sick, and there's no substitute teacher yet," Jessica suggested. "That would be great."

"Hey, everyone, what's up?" Elizabeth asked as they joined their classmates outside the classroom door.

"We have a new classmate," Amy Sutton answered. "Danny Jackson is in our homeroom now."

"You're kidding!" Jessica exclaimed. "He'd better not sit behind me."

"I don't think he'll get away with much. You know how strict Mr. Davis is," Elizabeth said.

"That's right, I am," Mr. Davis said, suddenly coming up behind Elizabeth. "Now would you all mind joining me *inside* the classroom?"

Elizabeth felt herself blush. She filed silently into the room with the others. She took her usual seat behind Amy and looked around.

Danny was sitting in the front row; Elizabeth figured that had probably been Mr. Davis's idea. Danny was talking quietly to the boy sitting next to him. He wasn't bothering anybody yet, but Elizabeth couldn't help wondering how long that would last.

"The legislative branch of our government is made up of the House of Representatives and the Senate," Mrs. Arnette said. "Now, every state . . ."

The teacher went on, but Jessica stopped listening. She sighed. *How boring*, she thought, glancing around the classroom. Danny was in Jessica's social studies class now. Fortunately, he was sitting three rows away from her. *That ought to be a safe enough distance*, Jessica thought.

Caroline had told Jessica that Mr. Clark, the principal, thought it would be a good idea to give Danny a fresh start by assigning him to different classes.

"Can anyone tell me what a senator does?" Mrs. Arnette asked the class.

Lila Fowler raised her hand.

"Yes, Lila?"

"He votes on laws and bills and other stuff in the Senate," Lila said confidently. "I know, because my father's best friend is Senator McMahon." Lila was one of the wealthier girls at Sweet Valley Middle School, and she liked to remind everyone of that fact. Lila was also Jessica's best friend (after Elizabeth), and even though she could be awful sometimes, Jessica thought she was a lot of fun.

"That's right, Lila." Mrs. Arnette nodded. "Now, as you can see from this chart, the three branches of American government are connected by a principle known as checks and balances. Does anyone know what that means?"

"It means that no one can do anything because someone's always watching them," Danny said. "Kind of like school."

Aaron Dallas and Ken Matthews burst out laughing.

"Yes, well, something like that." Mrs. Arnette smoothed the hairnet she always wore. Just then the buzzer on the intercom that connected the teacher to the principal's office buzzed. Mrs. Arnette crossed in front of the classroom and answered the intercom.

"Yes?" she said. "All right, I'll be right there."

Mrs. Arnette turned back to the class. "I have to go to the office to take an important call," she told them. "I'll only be gone a moment. Why don't you all work on copying down the information on the board while I'm gone? No talking, and don't move from your seats. I'll be right back."

Once she was gone, Danny got out of his seat and walked up to the board. He smoothed back his short brown hair and said in a high-pitched voice, "Now, class, why do we take social studies? Because we need to know about the world *around* us, do we not? Because we are social beings!"

Jessica had to laugh. Danny was doing a perfect imitation of Mrs. Arnette.

Danny turned to the board. He picked up a piece of chalk and started sketching something.

"Hey, what are you doing?" Aaron Dallas called out.

"You'll see," Danny promised. He stood right in front of the blackboard so that nobody could see what he was drawing.

Jessica glanced at Elizabeth. Elizabeth shrugged.

After a few more minutes, Danny stepped back from the board. Now everyone could see his drawing. It was a woman with glasses, a creased mouth, and a big net over her head. She was holding her lesson-plan book and shaking her finger in the air. Above the picture, he had written "The Hairnet, which was Mrs. Arnette's nickname among the students.

Jessica giggled. Danny was pretty funny.

"Nice picture!" Aaron said.

"Thank you," Danny said, taking a big bow. "Eet ees my masterpiece," he said with a phony French accent.

Jessica heard footsteps approaching in the hallway. "Mrs. Arnette is coming!" she warned Danny. No sooner were the words out of her mouth than Mrs. Arnette appeared in the doorway.

Danny jumped in front of his drawing.

"Were you teaching while I was gone, Danny?" Mrs. Arnette inquired.

"Uh, no," Danny answered. He tried to erase the picture behind him with his shirt sleeve.

"Then please return to your seat," Mrs. Arnette instructed him.

Danny gradually edged away from the board and went back to his seat.

Mrs. Arnette put her hands on her hips as she stared at the blackboard. "This is not art class, Daniel," she informed him sternly. "I suggest you focus on the subject at hand."

"Yes, ma'am," Danny replied, but as soon as Mrs. Arnette looked away, he grinned at Ken Matthews.

"I'd like to go over last night's homework, the questions at the end of chapter seven in your textbook," Mrs. Arnette told them. "Please get your papers out. What did you have for number one? Elizabeth?"

"False," Elizabeth answered.

"That's correct. What about number two? Aaron?"

"False," Aaron said.

"Correct. Jessica, number three?" Mrs. Arnette asked.

"Uh, true," Jessica guessed. She had been too busy working on a new cheer for the Booster Squad the night before to finish reading the chapter.

"Jessica, number three was not a true or false question," Mrs. Arnette said with a frown. "Did you do the homework?"

"False!" Danny answered.

Lila giggled.

Mrs. Arnette cast an irritated look at Danny, who sank down in his seat. "That's enough, Danny," she said. "Jessica? We're wait—"

Just then the bell signaling the end of class rang.

"We'll continue tomorrow," Mrs. Arnette told the class. "Please study this chapter on American government carefully, and memorize the material we just reviewed. Be advised that there will be a quiz sometime this week."

"Whew!" Jessica said to Lila as they walked down the hall to their lockers. "That was a close one."

"Saved by the bell," Lila said. "Could you believe that picture Danny drew?"

"It was pretty good," Jessica said with a smile.

"I can tell Mrs. Arnette's *thrilled* to have Danny in her class." Lila snickered.

"He's definitely going to liven things up. That class is so boring! And now we have a stupid quiz coming up," Jessica said.

"Maybe we should study together this afternoon. You know, out by the pool at my house," Lila suggested with a smile.

"We'll bring out the radio, get some sodas and some cookies, maybe a magazine or two . . ." Jessica suggested.

"We'll get a lot done!" Lila declared.

"Exactly," Jessica agreed.

Two

◇

Jessica walked into science class and tossed her notebook on her desk. Science was her least favorite class, and her teacher, Mr. Seigel, didn't help. Danny Jackson walked in and sat down a few seats away from her. He had been switched into almost all of her classes!

"Hi, Jessica," Ellen Riteman said, taking her usual seat in front of Jessica. Ellen was a Unicorn and one of Jessica's best friends.

"Hi, Ellen. Do you know what we're supposed to do today?" Jessica asked.

Ellen shook her head. Then, noticing Danny, she gave Jessica a questioning look. "What's he doing here?" she asked.

"They changed his whole schedule around," Jessica said. "Don't ask me why, but he's in practically all of my classes now."

"Maybe he wanted to be close to you," Ellen joked. "Maybe he has a crush on you."

"That's not funny!" Jessica replied hotly.

"Why not? I think he's pretty cute," Ellen whispered.

"Maybe, but having him around can have a bad effect on your hair," Jessica said with a grin.

When the bell rang, Mr. Seigel clapped his hands together to bring the class to order. They quickly reviewed their homework, and then Mr. Seigel announced that they were going to start a new experiment the following week.

Jessica raised her hand.

"What is it, Jessica?" Mr. Seigel asked.

"What kind of experiment is it? Are we going to have to do something gross?" Jessica asked, wrinkling her nose.

"Well, it depends what you mean by 'gross,' " Mr. Seigel said, imitating Jessica's expression. "We're going to dissect worms."

"Yuck! That's exactly what I meant!" Jessica said.

"Well, I hope you'll get used to the idea, Jessica, because *everyone* in the class has to participate in this experiment," Mr. Seigel said while eying the entire class. "In the meantime, I'd like you to learn more about what it takes to run an experiment successfully. One of the most important things you must do is a lab report. If you don't write down any of the observations you make, then the experiment is wasted. So, I'd like you to prepare the sample lab report in your workbooks. You may work in pairs. For today, you can choose your partners. *I'll* assign partners for the actual experiment."

Ellen turned around. "Want to work together?"

"Sure," Jessica said. They moved their desks together and flipped to the sample lab report in their workbooks.

"This isn't too bad," Ellen said. "All we have to do is follow the directions and make up a sheet just like this one."

Jessica took out a sheet of notebook paper and began copying down the outline. "I wish we could choose our own partners all the time. I don't want to get stuck with you-know-who." She glanced over her shoulder at Danny, who was working with Ken Matthews.

"Yeah, I can just imagine what he'd do with a worm," Ellen remarked. "He'd probably put it on your chair or down the back of your shirt or something."

Jessica heard loud voices behind her and looked up. She turned around just in time to see Danny pick up the lab report he and Ken had been working on and rip it in half.

"I can't believe you just did that!" Ken yelled. He tried to take the pieces of paper away from Danny, who was holding them behind his back. Ken grabbed the paper, and it ripped again. Seconds later, he and Danny were wrestling with each other.

"Boys! Stop it!" Mr. Seigel demanded. "Right now!"

Ken and Danny kept right on fighting. Ken shoved Danny hard and they both landed on the floor.

"Ken! Danny! Stop it this instant!" Mr. Seigel grabbed hold of Ken's arm and pulled him away from Danny. "Get up, Danny," he said. Then, still holding on to Ken, he turned to the class. "I'm sure both Ken and Danny would like to apologize for disrupting the class. I know I can trust the rest of you to work quietly for a few minutes while I escort these two to the principal's office. I expect you to be finished with your assignment when I return."

Danny slowly stood up and brushed off some of the dirt on his clothes. Then Mr. Seigel took him by the arm, too, and marched both boys out of the room.

"Wow," Jessica said once they were gone.

"Wow is right," Ellen agreed. "They're going to be in big trouble when Mr. Clark hears what happened."

"I wonder what they got into such a big argument about," said Jessica. "It couldn't have been this stupid thing!" She pointed at the lab report.

"Maybe they were fighting over you," Ellen said, giggling. "Maybe they *both* want to be your lab partner!"

Jessica frowned. "Very funny," she said, sticking her tongue out at Ellen.

"I think your hair looks great!" Elizabeth told Julie. She, Amy, and Julie were eating lunch together in the cafeteria.

"So do I," Amy agreed.

"Thanks," Julie said with a smile. "I like it, too." She shook her head so that her hair swung from side to side.

"Has anyone been giving you a hard time about it?" Amy asked.

"Not really." Julie took a bite of her peanut butter sandwich.

"Good," Elizabeth said. "I thought some of the Unicorns would tease you about it."

"Actually, Lila did say she liked my hair—even if my ears were a little big. And Charlie Cashman asked me if I'd gotten run over by a lawn mower," Julie said with a giggle.

"I thought you said people weren't giving you a hard time!" Amy said.

Julie shrugged. "I don't care. I like my hair this way. In fact, I might even thank Danny for forcing me to get it cut." She wrinkled her nose. "Well, on second thought . . . maybe not."

Elizabeth pulled some chocolate chip cookies out of her lunch bag and offered them to her friends. "Jessica and I made these last night. Actually, I made them and Jessica helped by eating a lot of the batter." Elizabeth grinned. "She told me that I'd have fewer cookies to bake that way."

"There she is now," Amy said, pointing at the lunchroom door with her straw. "Look. She's coming this way."

"Hi, Liz!" Jessica said cheerfully. "Can I borrow your notes for— Hi, Julie!" she said, noticing Julie for the first time. "How's it going?"

She casually took a few steps backward to get a better look at the back of Julie's head.

"OK, I guess," Julie said. "How are you?"

Jessica didn't reply for a minute. She was still standing behind Julie, surveying her head. "What did you say?" she asked absently.

"Jess!" Elizabeth cried.

"What?" Jessica asked.

"Stop staring!"

"Oh, was I staring?" Jessica asked innocently. "It's just that I can't get over your new haircut, Julie. I heard that Danny practically ruined your hair."

"It was just kind of uneven," Julie told her. "The woman who cuts my mom's hair evened it out."

Jessica shook her head in amazement. "Boy, she did a great job."

"Well, thanks," Julie said shyly.

"Have you heard the latest about Danny?" Jessica asked, grabbing a cookie from Elizabeth's bag.

"What did he do now?" Amy asked.

"He got into a huge fight with Ken Matthews in science class. They were wrestling on the floor!" Jessica announced.

"You're kidding!" Elizabeth put down her carton of milk and stared at Jessica. "How could anyone possibly get mad at Ken? He's one of the nicest guys in the whole school."

"Well, Julie's nice, too, but it didn't stop Danny from cutting her hair," Amy pointed out.

Jessica shrugged. "I don't know what they were fighting about, but they both got sent to Mr. Clark's office." She glanced around the lunchroom. "And I don't see either of them here, so they must still be in his office."

"If they didn't get suspended," Elizabeth added. "What's going on with Danny lately? I know he likes to clown around, but he doesn't usually pick fights with people."

"You have to admit, most of the boys in the sixth grade are pretty immature. Look at them." Amy pointed across the lunchroom to a tableful of sixth-graders. Tom McKay was balancing a cube of lime gelatin on his tongue, and Pete Stone had two straws sticking out of his ears. He was pretending to be deaf.

Elizabeth nodded. "I know what you mean. I hope he doesn't end up in really big trouble, though. The track team needs him."

"Are you guys going to the meet?" Julie asked.

"The Boosters will definitely be there," Jessica said. "In fact, I've been working on some new cheers."

"Great!" Amy said. "We're practicing this afternoon, right?" The Booster Squad was a cheering team that the Unicorns had started. Amy was the only Booster who wasn't a Unicorn or the friend of a Unicorn. The Unicorns hadn't wanted to let Amy join at first, but they had accepted her when it turned out that she was the best baton twirler in the entire school.

"Four o'clock at the football field," Jessica said.

"Sounds good," Amy said. "What about you, Elizabeth? Are you going to the meet?"

"I'm covering it for the *Sixers*," Elizabeth said. "It should be a good one. Danny told me I shouldn't miss it, because he was going to do something exciting."

"He's probably going to put itching powder in the other team's uniforms," Amy said.

"I don't think Danny fools around when it comes to track," Elizabeth said. "I wouldn't be surprised if he ended up in the Olympics someday."

"There's Danny now," Jessica observed.

Danny walked over to the table of sixth-grade boys and sat down next to Jim Sturbridge. Ken came into the lunchroom right behind him.

"Looks like they made up already," Amy said as the two boys sat down next to each other at the table.

"They didn't get suspended, either," Jessica said.

"So the track team still has a chance against Pinecrest," Elizabeth added with a grin.

Three

◇

There were so many people at Sweet Valley's track meet against Pinecrest that the bleachers were completely filled. The Boosters were standing in front of the bleachers, twirling their batons and doing the Sweet Valley school cheer. Elizabeth smiled as she watched Jessica jump up and down enthusiastically.

"Elizabeth!" Belinda Layton called to her from the stands. Belinda was a Unicorn and a friend of Elizabeth's. She loved sports, and was the star pitcher on a little league team.

Elizabeth waved to Belinda and slowly started making her way up to where she was sitting. "Hi! Did I miss anything?" Elizabeth asked.

"The first two races," Belinda told her. "Pinecrest is beating us, but not by much."

"Did Danny race yet?" Elizabeth asked.

"No," Belinda replied. "But I think he's about to." She pointed to the track, where Danny was lined up with five other runners.

"This must be the eight hundred meter then," Elizabeth said. "I'm glad I got here in time! I'm covering the meet for the *Sixers*."

Suddenly the starter called out, "On your marks . . . get set . . . GO!"

Elizabeth stood on her tiptoes so that she could see the track better. Danny immediately took about a fifteen-yard lead over the second place runner from Pinecrest. By the time Danny had circled the track one complete time he had stretched his lead even farther. When he passed in front of the bleachers, everyone started yelling his name.

"Way to go, Danny!"

"Leave 'em in the dust, Jackson!"

"All right, Danny!" Elizabeth cried.

Danny seemed to run even faster on his second lap around the track. When he finished, he was almost half a lap ahead of everyone else.

Coach Stern ran over as Danny crossed the finish line. He showed Danny a stopwatch, and then threw his arm around Danny's shoulders.

"I think he set a school record!" Elizabeth said eagerly. "I have to go talk to him."

"See you later," Belinda said.

When the last runner passed the finish line, Elizabeth crossed the track and hurried over to Danny. "Congratulations! Great race!" she told him.

"Thanks." He pulled sweat pants on over his shorts. "I have to keep my muscles warm in between races," Danny explained.

"I told you that I'm writing another article for the *Sixers*, right?" Elizabeth asked.

Danny smiled. "Make sure you mention that I just broke the school record."

"I thought so!" Elizabeth exclaimed. "That's terrific. Wait—didn't you hold the first record?"

Danny nodded, his brown eyes shining with excitement.

"How much faster did you run this time?" Elizabeth asked.

"Two point six seconds," Danny replied. "It probably doesn't sound like much, but for this distance it's a lot to take off your time."

Elizabeth started jotting down notes on her small memo pad. "There's something I've been meaning to ask you. When did you start running?" she asked.

"About two years ago," Danny replied.

"What got you interested in track?"

Danny shrugged. "I started running because I kept getting crushed in football. I figured if I could run fast enough, I'd be a great running back. If no one could catch me, no one could tackle me."

"Well, nobody can catch you now! Your parents must be really proud of you," Elizabeth said.

Danny's smile faded. "I doubt it," he said quietly.

"What do you mean?" Elizabeth asked, surprised. "Of course they are."

"It's none of your business!"

"I'm sor—" Elizabeth began. But before she

could finish Danny turned and walked off toward Coach Stern.

Elizabeth watched him go. *Why did Danny get so angry all of a sudden?* she wondered. She turned to walk back toward the bleachers. She was so busy thinking about Danny that she didn't notice Jim Sturbridge sitting on a bench by the side of the track. Jim was on the track team, too. Elizabeth knew Jim pretty well because they were in the same homeroom.

"Hi, Elizabeth," Jim said.

"Hi, Jim," she said, startled by his voice. "Did you run yet?"

Jim shook his head. "Three more events, then I'm up."

"Danny did a great job, didn't he?" Elizabeth commented.

"Yeah," Jim agreed.

"Do you think we're going to win the meet? After all, Pinecrest is supposed to be one of the best teams around," Elizabeth said.

"Well, it will be tough," Jim replied. "But I think we'll beat them, especially if Danny can beat Mark Swanson in the next race. He's the best runner they have."

"I was just interviewing Danny for the *Sixers*, but he got mad at me," Elizabeth blurted out. "I said something about his parents and he told me to mind my own business. Doesn't he get along with them?" she asked.

"I think he does," Jim replied. "I've been over to his house a lot."

"Really? What are his parents like?" Elizabeth asked.

"They're scientists. I don't know where they work or anything, but I think they do some real high-tech research," Jim said.

"Wow, that's great. Do they ever come to Danny's meets? I didn't see any parents here today," Elizabeth said.

Jim shook his head. "I don't think they like sports much. Danny told me that they want him to quit running so he can spend more time studying," Jim said.

"I hope they don't make him give up the team!" Elizabeth said.

Jim nodded. "I know. We could never win without him."

"If Danny's parents came to one of the meets and saw him run, I'm sure they'd change their minds," Elizabeth said.

"Maybe," Jim said.

"Good luck in your race," Elizabeth said. "Not that you'll need it."

"Thanks," Jim said shyly.

As she walked back to the bleachers, Elizabeth thought about Danny. She was sorry that she had made him so angry, although she wasn't sure what she had said to make him feel that way.

"And Sweet Valley wins by five points!" Coach Stern announced over his megaphone.

"Yeah, Sweet Valley!" the Boosters yelled. The crowd cheered and applauded the team.

"That was close," Jessica said as she and Lila picked up their book bags and started walking toward the parking lot.

"I know!" Lila said. "I thought we were going to lose it for sure when Winston messed up." Winston Egbert had come in fourth in the four hundred meter. He usually did much better.

"What do you want to do now?" Jessica asked.

"We could go to Some Crumb and get some cookies," Lila suggested.

"That sounds great. I'm starving," Jessica replied. "It must be all the yelling we did."

"There's a jewelry store next to Some Crumb that I want to go to, too," Lila said.

"What are you going to get?" Jessica asked.

"Nothing today," Lila said. "I just want to look at their earrings."

"Why?" Jessica asked. "You don't have pierced ears."

"Not yet," Lila said smugly, "but I will soon."

"You're kidding!" Jessica exclaimed. The only girls she knew with pierced ears were in the seventh and eighth grades.

Lila smiled. "I asked my father if I could get them pierced and he said it was OK. But I'm waiting to find the perfect piercing studs first. I'm going to have to wear them for six weeks, so I want them to be gorgeous." Lila pulled her hair back from her ears. "What do *you* think, Jessica? Gold or silver?"

"How about diamonds?" Jessica muttered.

"Hmm . . . I'm not sure if I can wear them, but I'll find out," Lila said. "Great idea!"

Jessica loved being best friends with Lila, but sometimes she made Jessica furious. Lila was always the first to get everything—a horse, a stereo, her own phone, and now, pierced ears.

"Why don't you ask your parents if you can get yours done, too?" Lila said. "We could do it together."

Jessica didn't want Lila to know how excited she was by that idea just in case her parents said no. She didn't want to have to admit that she wasn't allowed to do something Lila could do. But if she acted indifferent and they said no, she could always pretend she had changed her mind.

"I'll think about it," Jessica said.

On Thursday, Mrs. Arnette gave Jessica's class the quiz she had warned them about earlier in the week. After Mrs. Arnette collected the quizzes, she reviewed the answers with the class. Jessica scowled. If she missed a question, she would have preferred to wait until the next day to find out about it.

"How about the last question?" Mrs. Arnette said. "How long is a senator's term in Congress? Danny?"

"Six years," Danny answered quickly.

"Correct." Mrs. Arnette smiled at him. "Good job."

Jessica shifted in her seat. *So much for that one*, she thought.

"OK, that's it. I'll correct your quizzes and return them to you tomorrow, although all of you should have a pretty good idea of how you did. Let's move on to our next section. We're going to focus on the American judicial system for the next few days," Mrs. Arnette announced. "Please get out your textbooks, and turn to page one hundred fifty-two."

Jessica grimaced as she flipped through her textbook to the section marked "The United States Judicial System." It sounded very serious, and very boring.

"Now, as you'll see from this chart," Mrs. Arnette continued, "the judicial system has many branches. It is extremely complicated, and you'll need to study this carefully before you can understand how it works."

Danny raised his hand.

"Yes, Danny?"

"There's another way to learn how it works. *The Citizens' Court*. It's on every day at five-thirty on channel twelve."

Mrs. Arnette did not look impressed. "Danny, I don't think watching television is the best way to learn about law."

"Why not?" he asked. "I've learned a lot watching that show. They use real cases, you know. The judge isn't an actor; she's a real judge."

"Yes, but—"

"Did you see the one about the dog who attacked the mailman?" Aaron asked Danny.

Danny nodded eagerly. "Wasn't that excellent? That mailman looked like he was crazy, didn't he?"

"Maybe the dog gave him rabies," Aaron said, laughing.

Mrs. Arnette clapped her hands together. "That's enough. Let's get back to our textbook. I'm sure your TV show will . . . supplement what you learn in my class," she said slowly.

"Mrs. Arnette, have you ever seen *The Citizens' Court*?" Danny persisted.

Mrs. Arnette frowned. "I have better things to do with my time. Now, I'd appreciate it if you would drop this subject," she told Danny with a stern look. "We've wasted too much time on it already!"

"So now we're going to waste our time on something else?" Danny joked.

"That's enough out of you, young man!" Mrs. Arnette snapped. "Be careful, or you'll find yourself in detention for your smart mouth. Is that clear?"

Jessica was surprised. Even though Mrs. Arnette was a hard grader, she almost never gave detentions. Danny had really made her angry. But *that* wasn't surprising. If there was a Detention Hall of Fame, he would be in it!

Four

◇

Jessica closed her eyes and tilted her face toward the warm California sun. It was Thursday afternoon, and she was sitting on the front steps of the middle school, waiting for Elizabeth to come out so that they could walk home together. Jessica wasn't paying much attention to the conversations going on around her—until she heard Bruce Patman's voice. She opened one eye and saw Bruce walking toward her with Jake Hamilton. Jessica thought Bruce was the cutest boy in the entire seventh grade. And Jake was definitely the best-looking guy in the eighth grade. Jessica decided to sit up so that she could get a better look at both of them.

"Let's go over to my house and play a couple of rounds of Video Master first," Bruce was saying to Jake. "Then we can meet the rest of the guys at Casey's."

"OK," Jake said, nodding. "Do you have the latest version?"

"Sure," Bruce replied. "Don't I always?" Along with being one of the cutest boys in Sweet Valley, Bruce was also the wealthiest.

Jessica sighed as she watched the two boys walk by. They hadn't even noticed her. She watched them continue down the sidewalk. They stopped to talk to a seventh-grade girl whom Jessica recognized as a member of the girls' track team. Jessica didn't know her name, but she had seen her run and had to admit she was a terrific athlete. She excelled in both the broad jump and the high jump.

"Hi, Jess," Elizabeth said.

Jessica turned around and was startled to find Elizabeth standing right behind her. "Hi, Lizzie. I didn't even hear you walk up." She got up. "Come on, let's go."

Bruce and Jake were still talking to the girl from the track team when Jessica and Elizabeth walked by.

"Think you can jump even higher next week, Chrissie?" Bruce was asking her.

Chrissie shrugged. "Probably. I've been going at least two inches higher in practice."

"It's hard to perform your best in a competition," Jake said.

Jessica frowned as she and Elizabeth walked past them. She was obviously invisible to Bruce and Jake, and that bothered her. After all, she was a member of the Boosters and the Unicorns. She couldn't understand why neither Jake nor Bruce had ever paid as much attention to her as they were paying to Chrissie.

"Maybe I'll start doing aerobics," Jessica announced a few blocks later.

"It's supposed to be fun," Elizabeth said.

"Do you want to do it with me?" Jessica asked.

"I don't think so, Jess. I'm kind of busy right now," Elizabeth admitted.

"All right, but we won't be identical anymore when I'm in great shape and you're not!" Jessica warned her sister.

"That's OK. I think I can handle it," Elizabeth replied, smiling.

School went by slowly the next day. Elizabeth couldn't wait for English class. For the last few weeks they had been concentrating on reading short stories. Elizabeth loved short stories; she had even written a few of her own.

She looked up and smiled as Jessica walked into the room. "Hi, Jess. What's up?"

"Oh, hi, Liz," Jessica said glumly.

"What's wrong?" Elizabeth asked.

"I'm so sick of Lila talking about getting her ears pierced," Jessica said. "She can't talk about anything else."

"When is she getting them pierced?"

"I don't know, but I hope it's soon," Jessica said, taking her seat behind Elizabeth.

Danny came into the room and quietly took a seat in the back row. Elizabeth was surprised that he was acting so subdued. *Maybe he just likes to give certain teachers a hard time*, she thought to herself. Everyone liked Mr. Bowman. He was such a good teacher that it was easy to sit through his class—even on Friday afternoon, when no one could wait for school to be over.

Just as the bell signaling the beginning of class rang, a very thin woman entered the room. She had an oversize canvas book bag swaying from her shoulder. Her wispy white hair was held in a bun, and she was wearing a white blouse and a plaid kilt. She walked over to the desk on tiny high-heeled shoes and set down her bag.

"Hello, children," she said. "My name is Mrs. Winderhoven." She made her way over to the blackboard and wrote down her name. "Mr. Bowman is not feeling well, so I will be your substitute teacher today. He has asked me to read this story with you." Mrs. Winderhoven went over to the desk and pulled a manila folder out of her bag.

"This is one of the shortest short stories ever written," Mrs. Winderhoven said as she handed sheets of paper to the first person in each row.

Elizabeth took one and skimmed it quickly while the rest were being passed back. It was definitely short—it was only two pages long.

"Before we begin reading, I'd like to remind you that every detail in a short story is significant. Pay attention to everything the writer says," Mrs. Winderhoven advised the class. She put on her glasses and peered at the class list. "Nora Mercandy, why don't you begin reading for us?" she said, smiling at nobody in particular.

"OK." Nora cleared her throat and began the story. Elizabeth liked listening to Nora read. Nora always tried to make the words come alive. It was almost like listening to a performance of the story.

After a few minutes, Mrs. Winderhoven held up her hand. "Very nice. Thank you. You're a fine actress, young lady."

A few of the kids in the class snickered.

"All right then . . ." Mrs. Winderhoven consulted the class list again. "Mr. Jackson, please continue. And try to put the same emphasis into it that our friend Miss, uh—"

"Mercandy," Nora said.

"Yes, exactly," Mrs. Winderhoven said. "Continue, please."

"Don't you think we should discuss what's already happened in the story?" Danny asked. "That's the way Mr. Bowman does it."

"Well, *I* am the teacher today. And I'd rather wait until we're finished and then discuss the story as a whole," Mrs. Winderhoven said. "We must *experience* the story first."

Elizabeth heard a few giggles behind her.

"We're waiting, Mr. Jackson," the teacher said.

Danny sighed loudly and leaned over his desk to get a closer look at the photocopy. "Uh, Mrs. Winderhoven?"

"Mmm? What now?" the teacher asked.

"I'll go ahead and read if you want, but I think you should know that there's a mouse under my desk," Danny said calmly.

"A what?" cried Mrs. Winderhoven.

Elizabeth turned around and looked under Danny's desk.

Danny made a scuffling noise with his feet. "A mouse. I just scared it away." He jumped up from his desk. "There it goes! Under the bookcase!"

"Oh, dear!" Mrs. Winderhoven stood up. She looked nervous. "Catch it, someone, will you?"

Tom McKay, Belinda Layton, and Danny all ran over to the bookcase by the window. Belinda kneeled down and tried to peer underneath it. "I can't see. It's too dark," she said.

"Maybe it got out already," Danny suggested. "Does anyone see it?"

"You mean it's still running around?" Jessica demanded, quickly folding her legs underneath her so that her feet were off the floor. "Get it!"

"Oh, I just hate rodents," Mrs. Winderhoven said. She kept glancing around her feet anxiously. "I'm going to get the custodian. Perhaps he can catch it. Stay calm, boys and girls!" she said as she rushed out the door and slammed it behind her.

"Can you see it?" Danny asked.

Belinda shook her head. "It must be way back there, or else it crept through a hole in the wall."

A few minutes later, one of the school's custodians opened the door. "What's going on here?" he asked. Elizabeth could see Mrs. Winderhoven standing behind him, staring at the classroom floor with a worried expression.

"We saw a mouse!" Tom announced.

"Actually, it was Mr. Jackson who saw it first," Mrs. Winderhoven said from the hallway.

"Yeah, it was right under my desk!" Danny said. "Then it ran over here. We think it's hiding under this bookcase."

"Move aside, kids," the custodian instructed them as he crossed the room. "You can go back to your seats now." Mrs. Winderhoven watched him from the hallway. The custodian crouched down on the floor and shined his flashlight under the bookcase. "Nope, nothing in here," he said. He stood up and brushed off his overalls. Then he walked around the room, looking around the baseboards and in all the corners. "What color did you say it was?"

"Um, it was brown," Danny said.

The custodian rubbed his chin with his hand. "That's strange. I've been working here for seven years, and we've never seen any mice before. I don't know why one would turn up now."

"Maybe this mouse escaped from the science lab," Belinda suggested.

"Yeah!" Danny agreed.

"No, those doors are all locked tightly," the custodian said. "Besides, those mice are white. Well, ma'am, I don't see any reason why you can't continue with your class. There's no mouse in this room, I can tell you that much."

Mrs. Winderhoven cleared her throat loudly.

"I see." She seemed much calmer all of a sudden. She came back into the classroom. "Thank you, sir. I am most grateful to you," she said.

"You're welcome. Glad I could help." The custodian smiled at her, then left the room.

Mrs. Winderhoven looked at Danny. "Young man, I will have no more disruptive incidents in my classroom. Do you hear me?"

"But there was a—"

"That's quite enough," Mrs. Winderhoven said sternly. "I have been teaching English for thirty-five years, and I have seen more than my share of high jinks. I will not tolerate unruly behavior. Where were we?" she asked.

"We had just finished reading the beginning of the story," Nora said.

"Yes, that's right." Mrs. Winderhoven pursed her lips and looked around the room. "You were doing such a lovely job reading, dear. Why don't you continue?"

"Hurray!" Jessica called, dashing out the front doors of the school. "It's the weekend!"

Elizabeth smiled at her sister as she followed her down the steps. "Free at last, huh, Jess?"

"Exactly!" Jessica giggled. "What are you doing this weekend, Lizzie?"

"I want to get started on my article about the track team," Elizabeth told her.

"It's the weekend!" Jessica exclaimed. "You're not going to work the whole time, are you?"

"No. I just want to get it started so I don't have to worry about it next week," Elizabeth explained.

"You have lots of time," Jessica declared impatiently. "Anyway, it doesn't look like the next meet will be very exciting," she added.

"What do you mean?" Elizabeth asked. "With Danny, and Jim, and Stuart Collins running, it's bound to be really exciting."

"Well, maybe for Jim and Stuart, but Danny's chances of competing are pretty slim. Didn't you hear what happened?" Jessica asked.

"No," Elizabeth replied.

"Well, you know what went on in English today, with the mouse," Jessica said.

"Of course. I was there," Elizabeth reminded her.

"Right. Well, anyway, when Mrs. Winderhoof—"

"Winderhoven," Elizabeth corrected her.

Jessica folded her arms across her chest. "Are you going to let me tell you the story or not?"

"Sorry. Go on," Elizabeth said.

"Well, I guess she went to the teachers' lounge after class and told a few of the other teachers what had happened. And one of them must have told Mr. Clark, because in the middle of science class, Danny got called to the principal's office," Jessica went on. "And Mr. Clark told Danny that if he gets into trouble one more time, he's off the track team *for good*. Boy,

I bet he's going to have a lot of fun next Tuesday, on Parents' Night," she added.

Elizabeth shook her head. "I guess not," she said. Parents' Night was the night when parents visited the school and discussed their children's progress with their teachers. Elizabeth remembered what Jim Sturbridge had told her about Danny's parents.

"How did you find out about all this?" Elizabeth asked.

"I overheard Danny telling Ken Matthews what happened when he came back into class," Jessica said.

Elizabeth played with the strap on her backpack, thinking. "Maybe he'll be really careful from now on," she said hopefully. "He practically lives for track. There's no way he's going to let himself get kicked off the team now."

"Want to bet?" Jessica asked. "Come on, Lizzie. When is the next meet?"

"About three weeks from now," Elizabeth said.

"Three weeks," Jessica said, shaking her head. "Danny can't stay out of trouble for three *hours*. He's not going to last three weeks without doing anything!" she predicted.

Elizabeth hoped her twin was wrong. Without Danny, the team couldn't possibly win!

Five

◇

Jessica flopped onto her bed and opened the bag of clothes she had just bought at Super Sports. She loved her new purple aerobic tights and the matching white T-shirt with swirls of purple, pink, and blue. She was glad baggy gray sweat pants were out of fashion.

Jessica reached for the exercise magazine she had also bought at the store and found the section marked "Fitness Test." "Are you a couch potato, or a lean, mean muscle machine?" the headline asked. The article began with a short quiz, which Jessica completed quickly. For ballet, she got ten points. She also walked at least two miles a day, and she got three points for that. She added up her score confidently.

"Half fit, half fat!" Jessica cried when she compared her score to the chart in the back of the article. "I can't be!" She went into the bathroom and stared at her reflection in the full-length mirror. She clenched her fist and tried to flex her biceps, but nothing happened.

OK, I'm not a weight lifter, but I'm not that bad off. All I need is a few workouts, and I will be a lean, mean muscle machine, Jessica thought determinedly.

She slipped out of her jeans and put on a pair of shorts and an old T-shirt. There was no use dressing up in her new aerobic clothes to work out at home, Jessica decided. She put her hair back in a ponytail, put on her sneakers, and ran downstairs to the living room.

"Hi there," Mr. Wakefield said, looking up from his newspaper. "Going somewhere?"

"Nope," Jessica replied, turning on the television. "It's time for *Jumping for Joy With June.*"

"Is that a new cartoon?" Mr. Wakefield asked.

"Dad! I'm too old to watch cartoons," Jessica said, rolling her eyes. Sometimes her parents acted like she was still in kindergarten. She changed the channel until a woman with a lime-green leotard appeared on the screen.

"Hello, everybody! I'm June! Are you ready to jump?" the woman asked brightly.

"An exercise show?" Mr. Wakefield said, sounding surprised. "I didn't know you liked that kind of thing, Jessica."

"Why don't you join me, Dad?" Jessica said. She started to move to the music, following June's motions.

"Uh, I don't think so," Mr. Wakefield said. "But you have fun!" He headed into his study and shut the door.

June moved from side to side, using different dance steps. Jessica had to concentrate to keep up with her. After ten minutes, she could feel a trickle of sweat running down her back. It wasn't exactly her idea of a perfect weekend activity, but the magazine said that if she wanted to get into top shape, she would have to make sacrifices.

"Jess, it's time to get up," Elizabeth said, shaking Jessica's shoulder on Monday morning.

"I'm awake," Jessica moaned. "I just can't get up."

"What do you mean? Are you sick?" Elizabeth asked.

"Not exactly," Jessica answered. "Here, help me up." She held out her hands and Elizabeth pulled her up to a sitting position. Jessica had done so many sit-ups and so much jumping over the weekend that she could barely move.

"Are you sure you're all right?" Elizabeth asked worriedly as Jessica walked stiffly over to her closet.

"I'm just a little, uh, sore from my workouts," Jessica admitted. "It's supposed to happen. You know—no pain, no gain."

Elizabeth couldn't help giggling at the sight of her sister hobbling across the room. "Be careful, Jessica. You could hurt yourself if you push too hard."

"I'm doing everything the magazine says," Jessica said as she picked out a sweater to wear to school. "Just wait, Lizzie. In a couple of weeks I'm going to look great."

"I think you look fine now," Elizabeth said.

Jessica remembered what the article had said about her: half fit, half fat. "I know," she told her twin, "but I'm going to look even better." She walked into the bathroom and turned on the shower.

"Hurry up or you'll be late!" Elizabeth said over the noise of the water.

"OK!" Jessica yelled back.

"What's the matter with you?" Steven asked. He laughed when he noticed the way Jessica was walking into the kitchen.

"Good morning, Mom and Dad," Jessica said, deliberately ignoring her brother.

"Good morning," Mr. Wakefield said.

"Where's Elizabeth?" Jessica wanted to know.

"She had to be at school early this morning. She said she'd catch up with you later. Do you want some pancakes?" Mrs. Wakefield asked.

"No, just some whole wheat toast for me," Jessica replied. Her magazine had said that natural grains made the healthiest breakfasts. She winced when she sat down at the table.

Mr. Wakefield noticed her grimace. "Too much jumping for joy?" he teased her.

"No, I'm fine," Jessica assured him. She decided to change the subject. "Mom and Dad, I've been meaning to ask you something."

"Uh-oh," Mr. Wakefield said. "Sounds serious."

"She wants to know if you'll wheel her to school today," Steven joked.

Jessica tapped her fingers on the kitchen table. "Very funny."

"What is it, honey?" Mrs. Wakefield put some bread into the toaster and sat down at the table with a cup of coffee.

"I want to get my ears pierced," Jessica announced.

"You do?" Mr. Wakefield said.

Jessica nodded eagerly. "I really, really want to. I've been wanting to for a long time. And now that Lila is getting hers done, I thought maybe we could go on the same day. It would be so exciting, and of course, I would pay for it out of my allowance."

"Didn't you just spend your entire allowance at the sports store?" Mrs. Wakefield asked.

Jessica frowned. She'd forgotten that. "Well, maybe you could give me an advance on next month's allowance," she suggested.

"How much does it cost?" Mr. Wakefield asked.

"You just have to buy the earrings they use to pierce your ears," Jessica said. "They're not very expensive."

"Well, Jessica, your father and I will have to discuss this later," Mrs. Wakefield said. The toast popped up and Jessica jumped up to get it. "I'm not sure this is a good idea," Mrs. Wakefield added.

"Why not?" Jessica asked. "Mom, everyone at school has pierced ears!"

"I don't think *everyone* does," Mr. Wakefield said.

"Every *girl* does," Jessica insisted, buttering her toast.

"Jessica, aren't you worried about all the blood?" Steven asked just as Jessica bit into her toast.

"Steven!" Mr. Wakefield said in a warning tone. "That's enough."

"It doesn't really hurt, does it, Mom?" Jessica asked.

"We'll talk about this later. Right now, you've got to get going. Why don't you take your toast with you? You can eat it on the way," Mrs. Wakefield suggested.

"Oh, all right," Jessica said, picking up her schoolbag. She knew she'd better not mention the subject any more that morning. She had a feeling convincing her parents to let her get her ears pierced was going to be difficult. But she was sure she could do it with a little time and patience. And for once, Lila wouldn't be the first one with something new!

Six

◇

"Pass the potatoes, Jessica," Steven said at dinner the next evening.

"What's the magic word?" Jessica asked, holding the bowl up in the air.

"Pass the potatoes *now*," Steven demanded.

Mrs. Wakefield cast a stern glance at Steven.

"Please," Steven mumbled.

"What time do you think we should leave for school?" Mr. Wakefield asked.

"I'm not planning on going until tomorrow morning," Steven said as he served himself a huge second helping of the mashed potatoes.

"It's Parents' Night at *our* school," Elizabeth informed her older brother. She turned to her father. "It starts at seven o'clock, so we should go pretty soon."

"Is that why you're both so dressed up?" Steven asked. "I thought you two were going on a double date or something!"

Elizabeth was wearing a white cotton shirt

with a lace collar and a denim skirt, and Jessica was wearing her new pale pink sweater dress.

"Very funny," Jessica said. "It just so happens we want to make a good impression on our teachers."

"It's a little late for that, isn't it?" Steven said.

Jessica folded her arms across her chest and glared at her brother.

"That's enough, Steven," Mr. Wakefield said. "Would anyone like another pork chop?"

"No thanks, Dad," Elizabeth said.

Jessica shook her head. "No, thank you. I think I'll go get ready." She tossed her napkin on the table and stood up.

"Me, too," Elizabeth said. "Should I clear the table first?"

"No, we have someone else in mind for that job." Mrs. Wakefield looked pointedly at Steven.

"But Mom—" Steven began.

"No buts about it," Mrs. Wakefield said. "We're all in a hurry to get to school, but you have lots of free time."

"Ha!" Jessica cried smugly. "So there."

"Jessica, just finish getting ready," Mr. Wakefield said. "We'll leave in a few minutes."

"I hope Mrs. Arnette doesn't tell them how I did on that last quiz," Jessica told Elizabeth once they were upstairs.

"How did you do?" Elizabeth asked.

"Never mind," Jessica said. "Look, if Mom

and Dad start to head into her classroom, distract them, OK?"

Elizabeth smiled as she followed Jessica into her bedroom. "OK."

Jessica stood in front of her mirror and brushed her hair. "I wonder if any seventh-graders will be there," she said.

"Are you thinking of anyone in particular?" Elizabeth asked.

Jessica shrugged. "No, I just think it's going to be really boring going around and talking to our teachers. It would be nice if there was something to look at."

Elizabeth laughed. "Parents' Night isn't supposed to be a boy-watching event, you know."

"Well, it should be," Jessica declared. "It would be a lot more fun than listening to everyone talk about our grades."

"Ready, kids?" Mr. Wakefield called up the stairs.

"We'll be right down!" Jessica yelled back. "Why did they have to invent Parents' Night, anyway," she muttered to Elizabeth.

"I can't believe so many people are here," Jessica said when the Wakefields walked through the front door of Sweet Valley Middle School. "You'd think they were giving away prizes or something."

"The school looks so nice," Mrs. Wakefield said. It was obvious that the teachers had been preparing all week for Parents' Night. The students' work was displayed in each classroom and students and their parents strolled up and down the hallways, meeting with teachers and talking to classmates. Mr. Clark was meeting parents in the gym. Fruit punch and cookies were being served in the main hall.

"Where should we go first?" Mr. Wakefield asked.

Jessica gave Elizabeth a look which said, *Anywhere but Mrs. Arnette's!* "How about starting with Ms. Wyler?" Elizabeth quickly suggested.

"Sounds good," Mr. Wakefield agreed. "Show us the way."

When she walked into her math classroom, Elizabeth was surprised to see Danny there with his parents.

Mr. and Mrs. Wakefield walked around the room, looking at the items displayed on the walls while they waited their turn to talk with Ms. Wyler. Elizabeth couldn't help overhearing the Jacksons' discussion with the teacher.

"Danny has done very good work so far this term," Ms. Wyler said. "I'm pleased with his progress."

"Then why is he only getting a B?" Mrs. Jackson asked.

"Well, he had a little trouble on a recent test," Ms. Wyler said. "We just started a section on word problems, and he seems to be having a hard time with those. I'm sure he'll pick it up soon. Many students have trouble grasping the concept of word problems. It's nothing to be concerned about."

Elizabeth glanced at Danny. He looked nervous. "I'll do better on the next test," he told his parents.

"Well, I certainly hope so," Mr. Jackson said.

Poor Danny! Elizabeth thought. It seemed as if his parents were very disappointed that he was getting a B.

"Thank you for your time," Mr. Jackson said to Ms. Wyler. The Jacksons turned to move on to the next classroom. Danny walked right past Elizabeth.

"Hi, Danny," she said.

Danny didn't answer. He looked so worried that she wondered if he had even heard her.

"Mr. and Mrs. Wakefield? I'll see you now," Ms. Wyler said cheerfully.

"Well, here goes nothing," Jessica whispered in Elizabeth's ear.

Elizabeth tried not to giggle when she saw Mr. Bowman. He had a reputation for his brightly colored, mismatched outfits, and tonight was no exception. He had on a black-and-green plaid jacket, an orange tie, and bright blue trousers.

Jessica poked Elizabeth in the ribs. "We should grade Mr. Bowman on his clothes," she said. "He gets an F from me."

"I'd give him an A, for originality," Elizabeth said.

Jessica rolled her eyes.

"Where did Mom and Dad go?" Elizabeth asked.

"I think they ran into someone they know in the hallway." Jessica shrugged. "It's fine with me if they stay out there all night."

"You can't avoid Mrs. Arnette forever," Elizabeth said. "Besides, she's not going to talk about that one quiz the whole time."

"I hope not!" Jessica exclaimed. "Look, there's Lila." Jessica ran over to her friend, who was standing in the classroom across the hall.

Elizabeth walked up to Mr. Bowman. "Hi," she said. "My family deserted me."

Mr. Bowman laughed. "Well, since they're not around, let's talk about the next *Sixers* edition." Mr. Bowman was the faculty adviser for the newspaper. "How's the piece on the track team going?" he asked.

"OK," Elizabeth said with a smile. "I've almost finished it."

"Good." Mr. Bowman nodded. "What do you think you'd like to work on next?"

"I thought I might write about the new youth center downtown," Elizabeth said.

"That sounds like a very good idea," Mr. Bowman said.

Just then Mr. and Mrs. Jackson walked into the room with Danny.

"Hello, Danny," Mr. Bowman said. "It's a pleasure to meet you, Mr. and Mrs. Jackson. I'm glad you could make it this evening." He shook their hands and then turned to Elizabeth. "Would you excuse us, Elizabeth?"

"Sure," Elizabeth replied, stepping out of their way.

Mr. and Mrs. Wakefield came up to the doorway. "Sorry to keep you waiting, honey," Mrs. Wakefield said. "We got into a conversation with the Knoxes."

"I don't think I've ever met them. Who are they?" Elizabeth asked.

"Mrs. Knox is an assistant district attorney, so I know her from court," Mr. Wakefield explained. "Where did your sister go?"

Elizabeth pointed across the hall. Mr. Fowler was busy talking to a teacher, and Jessica and Lila were sitting in the back of the room talking.

"I'll go get her," Mr. Wakefield said. "Maybe Mr. Bowman will be ready for us by the time we come back."

The Jacksons had been talking quietly with Mr. Bowman, but suddenly the noise in the hallway died down and Elizabeth could hear them clearly.

"Danny makes excellent contributions to our class discussions," Mr. Bowman said. "But he needs to be more careful about preparing his homework assignments."

"I think he'd be much better off if he gave up track," Mrs. Jackson commented. "Then he'd be able to devote more time to his studies."

"I agree he needs to spend more time working on his reading," said Mr. Bowman. "But I don't think that quitting the track team will do anything except make him unhappy. As you know, he's an exceptional runner. And extracurricular activities are very important to all our students."

"But Danny hasn't been doing well in English for quite some time now," Mr. Jackson argued. "Don't you think we should try something different?"

"What do you mean?" Mr. Bowman asked.

"Well, perhaps he *should* give up the track team," Mr. Jackson said, "so that he can concentrate on his homework assignments. He's obviously bright enough. He simply doesn't have enough time to do a thorough job of studying."

"Perhaps Danny just needs to rearrange his schedule a bit," Mr. Bowman suggested, "make some time during the day to get a head start on his homework."

They're talking about Danny as if he's not even in the room, Elizabeth thought. She looked at Danny, who looked as if he wanted to disappear. At least Mr. Bowman was sticking up for him. It was obvious that neither Danny's parents nor Mr. Bowman knew about Mr. Clark's threat to kick Danny off the track team. They were talking about him leaving the team as if it were going to be *his* choice. Elizabeth had a feeling that Danny hadn't told his parents about Mr. Clark's threat because they would have welcomed it!

"Penny for your thoughts," Mrs. Wakefield

said, gently touching Elizabeth's arm. "Is something wrong? You're so quiet."

Elizabeth smiled absently at her mother. "It's nothing," she said.

Danny felt as if Parents' Night had been going on for hours already, but when he looked at the clock it was only half past seven. At least most of his teachers had been pretty nice. So far, not one of them had mentioned the trouble he'd been in lately. They probably assumed that his parents had heard enough about it already. But the truth was, his parents didn't know what had been going on. Whenever they asked him how school was, he told them everything was fine. They always seemed satisfied with that answer.

"Well, I'm glad we had this chance to talk," Mr. Bowman was saying. "Thank you for coming by, Mr. and Mrs. Jackson."

Danny breathed a sigh of relief. Mr. Bowman hadn't mentioned how Danny had scared the substitute teacher, Mrs. Winderhoven, with an imaginary mouse. *What if my parents talk to Mr. Clark?* Danny thought as they said goodbye to Mr. Bowman.

The last time he had been called in to Mr. Clark's office, he had been given a note to bring home. Mr. Clark had told him that the note explained the situation at school and why he would be forced to take Danny off the track team if Danny didn't start behaving. Mr. Clark had wanted Danny's parents to sign the note and return it to him.

But Danny had signed the note himself. He had carefully copied his father's signature and returned the note to the principal's office. He knew he'd be in big trouble if Mr. Clark found out about the forgery, but he had to take that chance. He didn't want his parents to know what was going on at school.

But now they're going to find out for sure, Danny thought as they rounded the corner and headed into the gym. He spotted Mr. Clark standing inside by the windows, mingling with parents.

"It's awfully crowded in here," Danny said.

"I didn't realize there were so many students at this school," Mrs. Jackson said.

"Yeah, it's pretty big," Danny said, keeping an eye on Mr. Clark.

"I'd like to meet the principal," said Mr. Jackson. "I've heard good things about him."

Danny's heart started beating doubly fast. His worst fear was about to come true. If Mr. Clark mentioned the note, his parents would probably ground him for a long time.

"But it seems as though we might have to wait a while," Mr. Jackson continued. "At least a half hour. Mr. Clark's surrounded by people."

"It does look that way," Mrs. Jackson said. "And I have to admit, I am feeling a bit worn out from our day at the lab. What do you say we go home now?"

Thank you, Mom! Danny mumbled to himself.

"Is that all right with you, Danny?" Mr. Jackson asked.

Danny nodded. "Yeah. Actually, I want to get started on my next book report."

"All right, then, it's settled," Mrs. Jackson said with a smile. "I'm glad we came, though. This visit has really been worthwhile."

And I'm glad we're leaving! Danny thought. He had never imagined he would get off so easily. Now, if his luck would just hold until the big district meet, he'd be fine!

Seven

◇

"I can't go to the meeting this afternoon," Jessica told Lila and Janet at lunch on Wednesday. Janet Howell was the president of the Unicorn Club, and one of the prettiest and most important girls in the eighth grade.

"Why not?" Janet asked. "Don't tell me you have something to do that's more important than a Unicorn meeting!"

"I have to work out," Jessica told them.

Lila looked at Jessica as if she were crazy. "Did you just say you were going to work out?"

"Sure." Jessica shrugged. "What's the big deal?"

"No offense, Jessica, but you don't strike me as the type," Janet said.

"I just decided I wanted to get in better shape," Jessica said. "There's nothing wrong with that."

"That's funny. You don't look like you gained any weight," Lila remarked.

"I didn't!" Jessica said.

"Then why would you want to exercise?" Lila asked.

Jessica shook her head. Lila was one of the laziest people she knew. Lila wouldn't possibly understand why someone would want to improve her body with anything other than a tan, since Lila's idea of exercise was getting up to change the channel on the television without using the remote control. "Because it's fun," Jessica said.

"What do you do, anyway?" Janet wanted to know. "Aerobics? Jogging? Weight lifting?"

"Oh, I do practically everything," Jessica said. "It's called cross-training. Sometimes I ride my bike, sometimes I jog. . . ."

"Are you training for the next Olympics or something?" Lila asked.

Jessica sighed. "No. Look, I just can't make it to the meeting. I'm sorry."

"That's OK," Janet said. "We understand if you'd rather sweat than hang out with us at the Dairi Burger."

Jessica loved going to the Dairi Burger. All the high-school kids went there after school to socialize. But she had made a commitment to herself. She was determined not to be "half fit, half fat" anymore, especially not if it meant boys like Bruce were going to pay more attention to girls like Chrissie than to her. And if she went to the Dairi Burger, she'd probably eat an order of French fries and a double-thick chocolate milkshake. She was getting hungry thinking about it, and she had just eaten lunch! So far, all exercising was doing for her was giving her a bigger appetite.

"We'll tell you all about it tomorrow," Lila promised. "By the way, Jessica, do you think you can fit in a trip to the mall this weekend? Or will you be too busy working out?"

Jessica sat up straighter in her chair. "I definitely want to go to the mall! Count me in."

"Good. I need your opinion on the piercing studs I'm going to buy," Lila said.

"What do they look like?" Janet asked.

"They're gold, of course. But I can't decide what size I should get," Lila said.

"Are you going to get your ears pierced, too?" Janet asked Jessica.

"Uh, I'm not sure," Jessica said.

Lila crumpled up her lunch bag. "Did you ask your parents if you could yet?"

Jessica nodded. "I asked them a few days ago. They said they'd think about it and let me know."

"You know what that means," Janet said with a shake of her head. "N-O."

"I'm not surprised," Lila said with a smirk. "Jessica's parents never let her do anything."

"Well, I'm sure they're going to let me get them pierced," Jessica said confidently.

Janet flipped her brown hair over her shoulder, revealing a beautiful pair of dangling silver earrings with beads. "I just got these over the weekend," she said, fingering one of the earrings. "Do you like them?"

They were exactly the kind of earrings Jessica pictured herself wearing. "They're terrific," she said. "I love big earrings."

"Well, first you have to wear those boring little studs," Janet explained. "But then you can get into the good stuff!"

"I can't wait!" Lila said.

Jessica decided to ask her parents about it again at dinner that night. *Mom and Dad have to say yes, they just have to!* she said to herself.

"Hi, Mom," Jessica said, walking into the kitchen.

"Hi, Jessica. How was your bike ride?" Mrs. Wakefield was standing in front of the sink, rinsing a head of lettuce.

"It was OK," Jessica said.

"How do you feel?" Mrs. Wakefield asked.

"Great!" Jessica said. Actually, at the moment, she felt like collapsing in front of the TV.

"Good, because I could use your help making this salad. Would you mind peeling some carrots?" Mrs. Wakefield opened a drawer and pulled out the peeler.

Jessica took it from her and stood next to her mother at the sink. She didn't mind helping, since it would give her the perfect opportunity to ask her mother about her parents' decision.

"Mom, did you and Dad decide yet whether I could get my ears pierced?" she asked casually. "Because Lila is ready to make an appointment. You have to set it up in advance, so I thought if— "

"Hold on a second, Jessica. Your father and I *have* reached a decision," Mrs. Wakefield said.

"Really? What is it?" Jessica asked eagerly.

"Well, maybe we should wait until Elizabeth is here, since it's going to affect her, too. I'll tell you both at dinner." Mrs. Wakefield started breaking the lettuce into pieces and putting it in the big wooden salad bowl.

"Can't you give me a hint?" Jessica asked.

"Well, I think we've reached a decision we'll all be happy with," Mrs. Wakefield said. "I'm going to go upstairs and make a phone call. When you finish the carrots, start on the tomatoes. And let me know when the timer goes off for the chicken, OK?"

"Sure, Mom!" As soon as her mother was upstairs, Jessica put down the peeler and started dancing around the kitchen. She was going to get her ears pierced! Maybe she'd even schedule an appointment a day earlier than Lila's. That would show her!

Jessica pulled her hair back and looked at her reflection in the kitchen window. She was going to look great with earrings!

"We've given this a great deal of thought," Mr. Wakefield began. "And we've decided that both of you can get your ears pierced as soon as you're fourteen."

Jessica's fork dropped onto her plate. *"Fourteen?"*

"I hadn't even thought about it yet," Elizabeth said.

"Well, Jessica's anxious to get hers done now," Mrs. Wakefield explained. "But I think you're too young. I didn't get my ears pierced until I was eighteen, you know."

"But Mom, things were different back then," Jessica argued. "I told you, everyone at school has them."

"My friends don't," Elizabeth said. "Except for Nora."

"I'll be in high school by the time I get to wear earrings," Jessica complained.

"That's right," Mr. Wakefield said.

"I'll be the last one in my whole class," Jessica went on.

"Come on, Jessica, it's not the end of the world," Mrs. Wakefield said.

Yes it is, Jessica said to herself. *Lila is never going to stop teasing me now.*

"Well, this is good news for me," Steven said. "Now I know I can get my ears pierced any time I want to!" He had just turned fourteen a few months ago.

Everyone started laughing except Jessica. She didn't see what was so amusing about being treated like an eight-year-old.

Eight

◇

Elizabeth wanted to go over her track team article with Danny during lunch period on Friday, but she couldn't find him anywhere. He wasn't in the lunchroom, and he wasn't outside. Finally, she decided to try the library.

"Hi, Mrs. Luster," she said to the school librarian.

"Hello, Elizabeth," Mrs. Luster said, smiling. "Can I help you with something?"

"I'm looking for Danny Jackson. Have you seen him?" Elizabeth asked.

"Yes, as a matter of fact, I have," Mrs. Luster said. "He's in the AV room, watching a video."

"Thanks!" Elizabeth said.

"He just got here, so if you want to join him, you probably haven't missed any of the movie," Mrs. Luster said.

"I think I will," Elizabeth said. She headed for the audio-visual room, knocked once, then walked in. Danny was lying on the floor, taking notes as he watched the movie. "Hi, Danny," Elizabeth said timidly.

Danny looked up. "What are you doing here?" he asked gruffly.

"I'm sorry to bother you, but I was wondering if you could go over my *Sixers* article with me. I want to make sure I have all the facts straight," Elizabeth told him.

Danny hit the "pause" button on the VCR and got to his feet. "Sure. Let's go out into the main room."

"What movie are you watching?" Elizabeth asked as they walked to a desk and sat down.

"*The Red Pony*," Danny said.

"I love that book," Elizabeth said. "How's the movie?"

Danny shrugged. "It's OK."

"Are you watching it for an assignment, or just for fun?"

"For fun," Danny replied. He sounded angry. Obviously, he didn't appreciate being interrupted.

"Well, uh, here's the article," Elizabeth said, pulling it out of her notebook. "I just need to know if I got everything right."

Danny took the sheet of paper and skimmed it quickly. "It's fine," he said.

"Even where I quote you?" Elizabeth asked.

Danny stared blankly at the paper and didn't say anything for a few minutes.

Elizabeth leaned over and pointed out the quote. "Right here."

"I know where it is!" Danny snapped. He moved the article closer to him and looked it over again.

As Elizabeth watched Danny, she noticed that he was straining to make out some of the words. It seemed to be taking him a long time to read the short quote.

Suddenly, she remembered Mr. Jackson saying on Parents' Night that Danny had always had trouble with English. *Maybe he just isn't a good reader*, Elizabeth thought. Once she started to think about it, Elizabeth realized she couldn't remember ever hearing Danny read aloud in class. Every time he had been called on, something had always come up that kept him from reading.

The last time he had been asked to read in social studies, Danny had told Mrs. Arnette he didn't feel well and he had gone to the nurse's office. Then there was the time he had pretended to see a mouse in English class when the substitute teacher called on him.

Elizabeth glanced over at Danny, who was still struggling to read the article. It all made sense. Danny had been causing so much trouble because he didn't want anyone in Sweet Valley to find out about his reading problem! And now he was in the library watching the movie version of a book because he couldn't read well!

But how could that be possible? Elizabeth wondered. Danny was so smart; he always talked in class and he knew a lot of interesting things. He did well in math. But then she remembered Ms. Wyler had said Danny had been having trouble since they had started a new unit on word problems.

"Danny?" Elizabeth asked. She didn't know how to ask him if her hunch was right, but she felt she had to say something. *Maybe he needs someone to confide in,* she thought. Elizabeth wanted to help Danny.

"I told you, the article is fine," he said, passing it back to her. He stood up and started heading back toward the AV room.

"Wait, Danny. I have to ask you something," Elizabeth said.

Danny looked at her impatiently. "Now what?"

"Do you have trouble reading?" she asked. "Because if you do, I—"

Danny scowled. "Just leave me alone, will you?" he almost yelled. "Stop being such a pain!"

"I—I'm sorry," Elizabeth stammered. "I just thought you might want some help."

"Well, I don't want your help!" Danny cried. He picked up a sports magazine. "This is what I think of your stupid article!" he told Elizabeth. He ripped off the cover of the magazine and threw it into the air.

"Look, I didn't mean to upset you," Elizabeth said, backing away as Danny took an encyclopedia off the shelf, ripped out some of its pages, and threw it down.

"Just mind your own business from now

on," Danny said. "And if you ever tell anybody what you told me, you'll be sorry!"

Elizabeth was frightened. She had never seen Danny get so angry before.

"Daniel! Elizabeth!" Mrs. Luster cried, running out from her office behind the main desk. She shook her head when she saw the book Danny had damaged. "*What* is going on?"

"That's what I'd like to know," Mr. Clark said.

Both Elizabeth and Danny turned around, shocked. The principal had come into the library without either of them noticing.

"I heard the noise all the way down the hall," Mr. Clark continued. "And I got here just in time to see you tear the pages out of that encyclopedia, Danny. Would you like to explain what you're doing?"

Danny didn't say anything.

"Well, I can tell you what he did," Mrs. Luster said. "He threw that magazine against the wall, tore out pages of one of our most valuable encyclopedias, and—"

"I get the idea," Mr. Clark said.

Suddenly Elizabeth remembered Mr. Clark's warning: one more incident, and he was going to take Danny off the track team. "Mr. Clark, it was all my fault," she exclaimed. She couldn't tell him why she had gotten Danny so mad, but she had to accept the blame for what had happened.

"Oh, I doubt that very much." Mr. Clark shook his head.

"No, it's true!" Elizabeth insisted. "I asked Danny to help me with my article when he was busy studying. I shouldn't have interrupted him."

"Elizabeth, why don't you go down to the cafeteria and get yourself some lunch," Mr. Clark said. "Danny and I are going to my office for a little talk."

Elizabeth looked down at the floor as Danny gathered his books and walked out of the library with Mr. Clark.

It's all my fault that he's in so much trouble, she thought.

"Elizabeth! Lizzie!" Jessica cried.

Elizabeth was walking down the hall toward her locker after last period. She turned around, waved at Jessica, then kept walking. She wasn't in the mood to talk to anyone, not even her twin.

"Is it true?" Jessica asked, when she had caught up with Elizabeth. There were several Unicorns with her.

"What?" Elizabeth said glumly. She twirled the combination on her lock and opened her locker door.

"Is it true that Danny Jackson hit you with a book?" Jessica demanded.

Elizabeth shook her head. "No, it's not true."

"But you guys *did* have a big fight, didn't

you?" Lila asked. "I mean, the whole school knows about it."

"Yeah, Tamara Chase was in the library and she heard *everything*," Janet said.

"Everything?" Elizabeth asked. She hoped Tamara hadn't heard what she had said to Danny. If the Unicorn Club found out Danny couldn't read, the news would be all over school.

"Yes! He told you to shut up and mind your own business," Janet said. She sounded a little shocked.

"What did you do that made him so mad?" Jessica asked.

"Nothing." Elizabeth shrugged.

"Nothing?" Lila asked. "That's kind of hard to believe."

"Well, it's the truth," Elizabeth said. She was glad they didn't know the real reason he had gotten so angry. "He was looking at this article I had written about him for the *Sixers*, and I guess he didn't like what I said about him. I told him I'd change the article, but he didn't believe me." Elizabeth didn't like lying, but she had to come up with an excuse that would satisfy them.

"What did you write about him?" Ellen asked.

"Look, it was no big deal. Danny was just in a bad mood and he took something I said the wrong way," Elizabeth said. That was actually close to the truth.

"Some bad mood! He practically turned the

library upside down, according to Tamara," Jessica remarked.

Elizabeth shrugged. "I have a meeting to go to," she said. "I'll see you later." She closed her locker and started walking down the hall.

"Do you want to meet afterward so we can walk home together?" Jessica called after her.

"I don't think so," Elizabeth said. "I don't know how long my meeting will last."

"Who's your meeting with?" Jessica asked.

"Mr. Bowman," Elizabeth called back over her shoulder.

"Oh. Well, see you later then!" Jessica said. "And be careful, Liz. Danny might still be mad at you. With a temper like his, you don't know what he'll do!"

Elizabeth quickened her pace. There was only one person she wanted to meet with, and it wasn't Mr. Bowman.

"Come in, Elizabeth. What did you want to see me about?" Mr. Clark asked.

Elizabeth walked into the principal's office. "It's about what happened in the library today," she said.

"Please have a seat." Mr. Clark sat down and rested his arms on his desk. "Elizabeth, I want you to know that I do not hold you responsible for anything that occurred. Nothing will go on your school record. Mrs. Luster told me that you just happened to be in the wrong place at the wrong time."

"But I was *responsible*," Elizabeth argued. "I can't tell you why right now, but it was my fault that Danny got so angry. I said something that upset him."

Mr. Clark tapped his chin thoughtfully. "No matter what you said to Danny, he should not have reacted that way. I can't hold you responsible for *saying* something, when Danny was the one who destroyed valuable school property."

"But he wouldn't have done it if it weren't for me," Elizabeth argued.

"That doesn't matter. I'm sure you're aware of the fact that Danny has been causing quite a bit of trouble around here lately," Mr. Clark said. "This is just the latest in a long list of incidents."

Elizabeth nodded. "I know. But there's a reason," she said.

"I'm sure there is," Mr. Clark said. "I've seen students act like this before, and there usually is a very good reason. But until Danny tells me what's bothering him, I can't do anything except try to get him to stop acting this way. And that's why I told him that as of today, he is suspended from the track team, indefinitely."

Elizabeth's heart sank. "Don't you think he'll get even angrier if he can't be on the team?" she asked.

"I think it will convince him that he has to behave himself when he's at school," Mr. Clark replied.

Elizabeth was quiet. She couldn't think of

anything to say that would convince Mr. Clark, except the truth.

"Anything else, Miss Wakefield?" Mr. Clark asked.

Elizabeth stood up slowly. If only she could tell Mr. Clark what was really bothering Danny! But she knew Danny didn't want anyone to know about his problem, and she wasn't going to betray him. "Thanks for listening," she said.

"You're welcome. I appreciate your concern. You know, it's not often that a student comes into my office *asking* to get into trouble!" Mr. Clark laughed.

Elizabeth smiled weakly.

"Don't worry about Danny," Mr. Clark reassured her. "He'll work things out soon enough."

Elizabeth wished she could believe that.

Nine

◇

Danny walked over to the track and sat down on the field. *Well, so much for the district meet,* he thought. He pulled some blades of grass out of the ground and tossed them into the air.

But it is all my fault, I guess. I shouldn't have yelled at Elizabeth like that. Danny was truly sorry he had yelled at Elizabeth. He knew she was only trying to help him. But she had made him angry because she was right. Danny couldn't read well. He could read some things, but not enough to get by anymore. He had been hiding it from everyone for so long that he couldn't believe someone had actually figured out his secret.

Danny had been having trouble reading for as long as he could remember. The only way he'd been able to hide it from his teachers was by making jokes all the time. They were all convinced that he liked to kid around more than he liked to do schoolwork. Danny hadn't always been the class clown. At his old school, he used to try to read out loud in class. But it had been horrible. When he couldn't make out the words, he'd just mumble through them, and the other kids used to make fun of him. He hated the idea that anyone would think he was stupid, so he stopped trying to read.

None of his teachers had ever really become aware of his problem, either. They just gave him low grades and told him to work harder. Sometimes they recommended that he get a tutor, but they never pushed him.

Danny did well in some subjects, like math and art, but reading was very difficult for him. Sometimes he felt like he was normal, even smart. But when he tried to read his textbooks he felt stupid. Sometimes he spent hours trying to read a single page. Now he was too far behind to catch up.

"Hey, Danny!"

Danny looked up and saw Jim Sturbridge jogging toward him. "Hi, Jim. How's it going?"

"I just heard you're off the team," Jim said. "I'm really sorry."

"Me, too." Danny tried to smile, but he couldn't.

"We'll never win the meet now," Jim said. "Do you think maybe Mr. Clark will reconsider after a couple of days?"

"I don't think so," Danny said. "He was pretty mad."

"Well, stay in shape just in case he changes

his mind, OK?" Jim started to jog over to where the rest of the boys on the team were standing.

"Yeah, sure," Danny mumbled. He would keep running, but he knew he wasn't going to get back on the team. Mr. Clark had made that very clear. He wondered if another note was going to be sent home to his parents. What if it was sent directly to them in the mail?

Danny stood up and started walking home. It occurred to him that he had someone besides Mr. Clark to worry about. He hoped Elizabeth wouldn't tell anybody what she had discovered.

Elizabeth rolled over onto her back and hugged her pillow to her chest. She felt miserable. She still couldn't believe her fight with Danny had gotten him kicked off the track team.

There was a loud knock at the door, and Jessica marched into the room. "Can I look at your notes from English?" she asked.

"Go ahead," Elizabeth said quietly.

"Where are they?" Jessica asked.

Elizabeth slowly swung her feet over the edge of the bed and sat up. Then she walked to her desk and took a notebook out of her backpack. "Here," she said, handing it to her sister.

"What's wrong with you?" Jessica asked. "You're acting like you lost your best friend."

Elizabeth flopped back onto her bed. "It's nothing."

"Oh, I know! You're still getting over the shock of having Danny throw books at you."

Jessica sat down on the edge of the bed. "I'm glad he got kicked off the track team. He deserves it."

"No, he doesn't," Elizabeth said quietly.

"What are you talking about? He could have hurt you!" Jessica exclaimed.

"He wasn't trying to hurt me," Elizabeth explained. "He was just angry, that's all. And it was my fault he got so angry."

"Why? Because you wrote an article about him that everyone in the sixth grade is going to read?" Jessica frowned. "Elizabeth, he should have thanked you for putting his name in the paper. Instead he tried to kill you!"

"He wasn't mad about the article," Elizabeth mumbled.

"What?" Jessica leaned closer to her twin, who was lying on her stomach.

"I said, he wasn't mad about my article." Elizabeth turned over and sat up.

"Then what was he so mad about?" Jessica clapped her hands together. "I know. He asked you out, and you turned him down! That's why he—"

"No, Jess." Elizabeth sighed. She wasn't sure if she should tell Jessica the truth or not. She wasn't used to keeping secrets from her sister, but she was afraid that if she told anyone about Danny's problem, it would get all over school. Then Danny would never speak to her again. Still, she had to tell *someone*. *Maybe Jessica will help me figure out a way to help him*, she thought.

"Well?" Jessica prompted.

"Do you promise not to tell anyone what I'm about to tell you?" Elizabeth asked.

Jessica nodded quickly.

"I mean it, Jess. You can't tell *anyone*. Not Lila, or Janet, or *any* of the Unicorns, or anyone else at school. If you do, I'll never forgive you," Elizabeth said seriously.

Jessica seemed to be thinking it over for a minute. "OK, Elizabeth. I promise I won't tell anyone."

Elizabeth hesitated. "I want it in writing," she said.

"Lizzie!" Jessica cried. "Don't you trust me?"

Elizabeth wrinkled her nose. "Well . . ."

"OK, OK." Jessica opened the notebook she was holding and carefully wrote down the date. Underneath the date, she wrote: "I promise I won't tell ANYONE Elizabeth's secret about Danny." Then she and Elizabeth both signed it. Elizabeth tore out the piece of paper and posted it on her bulletin board.

"*Now* will you tell me?" Jessica asked.

Elizabeth sat back down on the bed. "The reason Danny got so mad was because of something I said. But it didn't have anything to do with track or my article." She paused for a minute. "Jess, I found out that Danny barely knows how to read."

Jessica looked puzzled. "What do you mean, he barely knows how? He's in the sixth grade, isn't he? Everyone in our class knows how to read."

"Except Danny," Elizabeth said.

"Really? So you mean when you figured it out, he went crazy and started throwing stuff all over the library?" Jessica asked.

"Yeah. That's the whole story."

"Wow," Jessica said. "But I don't understand how his teachers don't know. I mean, I get a few things wrong on a test and they ask to see me after class. He must do a lot worse than I ever did."

"He probably does," Elizabeth said. "But remember how Danny saw that mouse in English class?" she asked. "I think every time he gets called on to read in class, he finds a way to get out of it. I don't think his teachers know that he has trouble reading."

"Then you're smarter than the teachers." Jessica laughed. "Good for you, Lizzie."

Elizabeth tried to smile. "This is serious, Jess," she said. "Danny won't admit he has a problem, and now he's been kicked off the team. What's going to happen to him next?"

"I don't know, Liz, but if I were you, I wouldn't get involved, not if Danny's going to go crazy every time you try to talk to him," Jessica said.

"But someone has to help him," Elizabeth argued.

"I can't believe he can't read," Jessica mused. "He's actually pretty smart. Boy, I hope they don't kick him out of school when they find out. Classes would be so boring without him."

"They wouldn't kick him out of school, Jess. They'd teach him to read better." Elizabeth sighed.

"Cheer up, Lizzie," Jessica said. "It's not your problem, you know."

After Jessica left the room, Elizabeth lay back down on her bed and stared at the ceiling. *It isn't my problem, and that's what makes it so hard!* she thought. *I can't do anything to fix it.*

Later that afternoon, Elizabeth went downstairs in search of her father. "Dad, can I talk to you for a minute?" she asked when she found him in his study.

"Come sit down," Mr. Wakefield said. "What's up?"

"I need to ask your advice about something," Elizabeth said.

"Go ahead." Mr. Wakefield leaned back in his chair.

"I'm not sure how to say this." Elizabeth paused. "I know somebody at school who's having a problem."

"What sort of problem?" Mr. Wakefield asked.

"Do you promise to keep this conversation confidential?"

Mr. Wakefield tapped his head. "I'll put it in my confidential file, OK?"

Elizabeth smiled. "OK. It's this boy who's in some of my classes at school. I asked him to look at this article I had written. But when I gave it to him, I could tell just by watching him that he couldn't read it."

"He couldn't read some of it, or he couldn't read all of it?" Mr. Wakefield wanted to know.

"I think he made out some of the words. But when I told him to look at a specific thing, he couldn't find it," Elizabeth explained. "I asked him whether or not he could read. I guess that was the wrong thing to do because he blew up at me."

"That's understandable," Mr. Wakefield said. "If he really does have a problem, he'd probably be pretty defensive about it. Maybe he has some sort of learning disability."

Elizabeth hadn't thought of that. She'd just assumed that Danny's last school hadn't been a very good one. "Do you think so, Dad?"

"It's possible," Mr. Wakefield said.

"What should I do? I know he doesn't want me to tell anyone about his problem. But he's in a lot of trouble at school," Elizabeth said. "If the teachers knew what was wrong, I think he wouldn't be in so much trouble. Does that make any sense?"

Mr. Wakefield was silent for a minute. He seemed to be thinking it over. "Elizabeth, I don't think there's anything you can do. If you go to your friend's teachers, you'll be betraying a confidence. I think you'd better wait until he decides to do something about it on his own."

"But he might *never* do anything!" Elizabeth said in frustration.

"Maybe he won't right away," Mr. Wakefield said. "But sooner or later, he'll have to. You can't help someone unless they want to be helped, Elizabeth. Believe me."

"OK, Dad, I'll wait," Elizabeth said. "But it's not going to be easy to keep this a secret."

"When your friend finds someone he trusts, he'll tell them what's going on," Mr. Wakefield said.

That thought made Elizabeth more hopeful. Maybe Danny would tell Mr. Bowman about his problem. They seemed to get along, and Mr. Bowman was very easy to talk to. "Thanks, Dad."

"Hang in there, Elizabeth. Things will work out for the best," Mr. Wakefield said.

"I hope so," Elizabeth said as she turned to leave.

Ten

◇

Jessica ran down the stairs and into the kitchen. She loved Saturdays. She wouldn't have to worry about doing her homework until Sunday night and meantime, she had the whole day free to spend at the Valley Mall with Lila.

Lila would probably have to look at every pair of earrings at the mall, but it would still be fun.

"Hi, Mom," Jessica said cheerfully.

"Hi, Jessica," Mrs. Wakefield said. She turned around from the stove. "I'm making french toast. Would you like some?"

"Yum! Definitely," Jessica said. She sat down at the kitchen table and poured herself a glass of orange juice. Another good thing about Saturdays was that her mother had time to make great breakfasts.

Elizabeth walked into the kitchen. "Good morning," she mumbled.

"Good morning, honey." Mrs. Wakefield smiled. "How about some French toast?"

Elizabeth sat at the table beside Jessica. "Sounds great. Thanks."

Mrs. Wakefield placed two plates in front of the girls. "Dig in," she said. "What do you two have planned for today?"

Elizabeth shrugged. "Nothing much."

"Lila and I are going to the mall," Jessica said. "I want to buy a couple of tapes."

"And Lila wants to buy everything else, right?" Mrs. Wakefield asked with a laugh.

"Actually, she's going to look at earrings," Jessica replied. She took a big bite of her breakfast. "This is delicious, Mom."

"Thank you."

"You and Dad haven't changed your minds about me and Elizabeth getting our ears pierced, have you?" Jessica asked hopefully.

"No, Jessica, we haven't," Mrs. Wakefield replied firmly. She put the orange juice back in the refrigerator.

"Don't you think that maybe you decided too quickly?" Jessica continued.

"Actually, we gave it a great deal of thought and the answer is *still* no," Mrs. Wakefield told her.

Jessica stabbed her fork into her french toast. She wasn't going to give up so easily.

"By the way, Jessica, before you go to the mall, there's something I want you to do," Mrs. Wakefield continued.

Oh, no! Jessica thought to herself. *I hate doing chores on the weekend.*

"You know what I'm talking about, don't you?" Mrs. Wakefield went on.

Jessica pretended she didn't understand what her mother meant. "No, I have no idea," she said innocently.

"It's about cleaning your room." Mrs. Wakefield sat down at the table with the twins. "You've promised to take care of it several times, but it's still a mess."

"But Mom, I told Lila I'd meet her at ten o'clock," Jessica protested. "I have to get the bus at nine forty-five. That's only an hour from now." There was no way she was going to spend her Saturday inside the house, dusting and vacuuming.

"Well, why don't you call her now and tell her you'll have to meet up later on," Mrs. Wakefield suggested.

Jessica pushed her fork around her plate. "But it'll take forever," she complained. "I'll be stuck inside all day."

"That's what happens when you put it off for so long," Mrs. Wakefield said. "Besides, it won't take all day if you work quickly. I'm sure you'll have plenty of time to shop with Lila."

"Can't I clean later, Mom?" Jessica asked. "I'll do it tonight."

"I think I've heard that one before!" Mrs. Wakefield shook her head and laughed.

Jessica stood up and slowly carried her plate to the sink. "All right, I'll do it now." She trudged up the stairs and into her room. The floor was covered with clothes, her desk was piled high with papers and cassette tapes, and she couldn't even see the top of her dresser.

Through the bathroom that connected their bedrooms, she heard Elizabeth walk into her room and turn on the radio.

"Lizzie, what are you doing today?" Jessica called through the bathroom.

"I'm meeting Amy and Julie later," Elizabeth answered. "That's it."

Jessica got up and walked into her sister's room. "Could you do me a huge, huge favor?"

Elizabeth looked at her suspiciously. "I'm not going to clean your room for you, Jess," she warned her twin.

"I don't want you to do it for me," Jessica said. "I was just wondering if maybe you could help me a little. For a few minutes, that's all."

"I don't know," Elizabeth said. She still sounded doubtful. "Whenever you ask me to help, it seems like I end up doing most of the work."

"Please?" Jessica begged. "I'll let you borrow my new workout clothes anytime you want to."

"Thanks," Elizabeth said, smiling at her sister's generosity. "But you look so sad I guess I have to help you."

"Thank you, Lizzie, thank you!" Jessica grabbed Elizabeth's arm and pulled her into her room.

"I'll sort your clothes if you start going

through that mess over there." Elizabeth pointed to a pile of magazines and notebooks in a corner that Jessica hadn't even noticed.

"I hate putting things away. I can never find anything when I do," Jessica grumbled.

"I think most of these clothes have got to go in the laundry," Elizabeth said, wrinkling her nose as she picked up a dusty purple T-shirt from under the bed.

Jessica cleared a spot on the floor and sat down. She picked a magazine off the top of the stack and started leafing through it.

"Jess, it's going to take forever if you read through every magazine," Elizabeth said.

"OK, OK," Jessica said. After she finished flipping through the first magazine, she dropped it in the trash can. Then she picked up the next one. It was a sports magazine and there was a very handsome man on the cover. Jessica opened the magazine. Elizabeth looked up from the pile of clothes she was sorting. "Jessica, I'm not going to help if you don't do anything," she commented.

Jessica glanced up from the article she was reading. Almost all her clothes were picked up. "Wow! Great job!" she told Elizabeth. "I'll get up in a second," she added. "I just want to finish this article."

Elizabeth sighed. "All right," she said. She began straightening the bedspread.

Jessica didn't want Elizabeth to be angry with her, so she hurried to finish the article. It was about Greg Voynow, a hurdler who had won a silver medal in the last Olympics. He had just set the world record at a meet in Europe. *He's adorable!* Jessica thought as she studied his picture.

She continued reading about the track star's life. Then she read something she couldn't believe. "You have to see this!" Jessica told Elizabeth. "This is really incredible!"

Elizabeth walked over and sat down beside her twin. "See what?"

"Look at this guy!" Jessica showed her the magazine.

Elizabeth skimmed the beginning of the article. "Pretty impressive," she agreed.

"He's great-looking, too, isn't he? But guess what? He didn't even know how to read until he was nineteen!" Jessica said.

Elizabeth looked very interested. "Where does it say that?" she asked.

"Right here." Jessica pointed to the paragraphs where Greg talked about his past. In the article Greg said he had gotten through high school because he was a good athlete, and all his teachers had wanted to pass him on to the next grade, whether he was ready or not. He had won an athletic scholarship to college, but the classes were more difficult there, and he had dropped out when he failed three classes in his first semester. Then, when he had tried to get a job, he hadn't even been able to fill out the applications. That was when he had decided he really needed help. At that point, he said, it didn't matter if he could run or not. He had found that if he couldn't read he couldn't get anywhere in life. So he had found a tutor to help him with his learning disability, and eventually he had gone back to college, where he had won the national championships and qualified for the Olympic team.

Elizabeth shook her head when she finished the article. "I can't believe this," she said. "I wonder if Danny knows about Greg."

"I'm sure he knows who Greg is, since he's so serious about track," said Jessica. "Greg Voynow just set the world record a couple of months ago."

"That's true." Elizabeth hugged her knees to her chest. "But I wonder if Danny knows that Greg also couldn't read when he was in school."

"Maybe we should leave this magazine in Danny's locker," Jessica suggested.

Elizabeth shook her head. "No, I've got a better idea. The article says that Greg lives in Santa Monica. I wonder if we could convince Greg to pay Danny a visit, in person."

Jessica shook her head. "I'm sure he's got better things to do with his time than that," she said. "He's pretty famous, you know."

"But it says in the article that he spends a lot of time at schools, giving speeches to students who are having trouble," Elizabeth said. "Maybe he'd come to Sweet Valley. I think I'll write him a letter and ask him."

"Well, you can try," Jessica said. "I wouldn't mind meeting him myself!" *Maybe he'll be im-*

pressed by what good shape I'm in, she thought. "How are you going to get his address?" she asked Elizabeth.

"I'll start by calling information," Elizabeth said. "He's pretty famous, so he might not be listed, but you never know." She stood up and brushed off her jeans. "Have fun at the mall."

"Wait a minute. Aren't you going to help me finish cleaning up?" Jessica asked.

"I want to write the letter now so I can put it in the mail today." Elizabeth smiled. "We've made a pretty good start. I'm sure the rest will go quickly." She walked out the door.

Jessica picked up the pile of magazines and dropped them into the trash can with a loud crash. Then she took everything that was on top of her dresser and stuffed it into the top drawer.

That should do it, she said to herself, looking around the room. She ran down to the kitchen and picked up the wall phone. Since Lila was being driven to the mall, Jessica knew she wouldn't have left yet.

One of the maids answered the phone. "Fowler residence," she said.

"Is Lila there? This is Jessica."

A minute later, Lila came to the phone. "Hi, Jessica. Are you still meeting me?"

"Yes, but I missed the last bus. The next one comes at ten forty-five, so I won't be there until eleven. Is that OK?" Jessica asked.

"Sure. If I get there early, I'll just start shopping," Lila said. "Actually, why don't you meet me at The Earring Tree?"

"All right." Jessica sighed. "See you there."

Elizabeth tapped her pen against the desk. She wasn't quite sure how to begin.

Dear Mr. Voynow, she wrote. *I read an article about you in* Sports Today *that made me want to get in touch with you. First, I want to congratulate you on holding the new world record. That's terrific.*

In the article, you mentioned having difficulty learning to read. Elizabeth paused to think. *I have a friend who can't read. We are in the sixth grade together at Sweet Valley Middle School. My friend is a great runner, and I know he'd love to meet you. I was wondering if you could talk to him about your problem. I think it would help.*

At the bottom of the page, Elizabeth signed her name and wrote down her phone number. She slipped the letter into an envelope and sealed it. Greg Voynow had actually been listed in Information, so she had gotten his address. She ran downstairs, got on her bike, and rode to the nearest mailbox. *I hope Greg is as nice as he sounded in the article,* she thought as she deposited the letter into the box. *And I hope he answers me soon.*

"How about these?" Lila held a pair of pearl earrings up to her ear.

Jessica shook her head. "Boring. Those are for old ladies."

"What about these?" Lila picked up a pair of rhinestones.

"They're OK." Jessica shrugged.

"I think I'll get the gold posts then," Lila decided. "I'm going to get my ears pierced next Saturday. Did I tell you that already?"

"About twenty times," Jessica mumbled.

"It's just that I'm so excited about it. Did your parents tell you yet whether you could get yours done?" Lila asked.

Jessica didn't want to tell Lila what they had said about waiting until she was fourteen. It was too embarrassing. "No, they're still thinking it over, I guess. But they said I could probably get them pierced soon." Two years wasn't exactly soon, but Lila didn't have to know that.

"Really?" Lila looked amazed.

"Mm-hm," Jessica said. "So what kind do you think *I* should get? I think silver looks best on me, don't you? Besides, we don't want to have the same earrings for six weeks."

"Your parents really said yes?" Lila asked.

"Sure," Jessica fibbed. "I mean, not in so many words, but they're leaning toward yes. I can tell."

"Does Elizabeth want to get hers pierced, too?"

"No, she says she's not interested," Jessica said. "Maybe I should get a necklace to match the earrings. What do you think?"

Lila didn't say anything. She took the gold posts and walked up to the cash register. She didn't seem so excited about buying her new earrings now.

Jessica smiled. She knew she couldn't fool Lila for long, but it was going to be fun while it lasted.

Eleven

◇

Jessica knocked once on Elizabeth's door, then walked in. It was Monday night, and Elizabeth was trying to finish her math homework. But she wasn't getting very much done. She couldn't stop thinking about Greg Voynow.

"Hi," Jessica said, sinking onto the bed. "What are you doing?"

"Math," Elizabeth said. "What about you?"

"I got to a good stopping point," Jessica said with a smile.

"You mean the beginning, right?" Elizabeth teased her.

"Actually, I can't concentrate. I keep wondering if Greg Voynow is going to call you. I'm waiting for the phone to ring."

"I didn't know you were so concerned about helping Danny," Elizabeth said.

"Of course I want to help Danny, Lizzie," Jessica said. "I'm interested in meeting Greg, too," she added casually.

"I wouldn't mind meeting him either," Elizabeth admitted.

"Could I look at that magazine again?" Jessica asked.

"Sure," Elizabeth said. It was sitting on the table next to her bed. She had been rereading the article earlier that evening.

Jessica flipped to the full-page photograph of Greg. "He's really adorable, don't you think? I love his hair."

Elizabeth nodded. "He is very handsome."

"And look at those eyes. Aren't they intense?" Jessica went on. "He should be a model."

"He probably doesn't have the time. Did you see that?" Elizabeth asked, pointing to a passage in the article. "He spends a lot of time talking to literacy groups and boys' clubs. And he works part-time at a children's hospital, too."

"He's amazing," Jessica remarked, still staring at his picture.

"I hope he calls." Elizabeth sighed.

Jessica turned around and stared at her. "Lizzie, you have a crush on him, don't you?"

"No, I don't," Elizabeth protested.

"Yes, you do!" Jessica insisted. "I can tell. I've never heard you sound that way before!"

Elizabeth had to laugh.

"Come on, Lizzie. You can tell *me*," Jessica said.

"Well, he *is* very handsome. And he seems like a really nice guy. I guess you're right. I do have a small crush on him," Elizabeth confessed.

"Wow, your first crush! Isn't it exciting?" Jessica asked.

"I guess so." Elizabeth shrugged.

"Just wait until you meet him. If you get really nervous, that means you like him a lot," Jessica told her.

"At this point, I just hope he calls me. I'm really worried about Danny," Elizabeth said. "He didn't say anything in class today, and he just glares at me whenever he sees me."

"Don't worry so much about Danny," Jessica said. "Besides, I bet when Greg reads your letter he'll call right away."

Elizabeth shrugged. "I don't know. I just told him the truth and asked for his help."

"Well, you're a good writer. I'm sure if anyone could convince him, you could," Jessica said confidently.

"I hope you're right," Elizabeth said slowly.

Jessica checked her watch. So far she had been running outside for eleven minutes. She was tired, but she wanted to keep going. She glanced down at her legs as she jogged. She loved her shiny purple tights. She thought they made her look like a professional athlete.

Jessica rounded the corner and turned into the park. It was fairly crowded, and she had to sidestep little kids and strollers on the sidewalk. It was getting harder and harder to lift her legs, but she was determined to run the loop around the park.

As she came up to the football field, she couldn't believe her luck. A group of boys from school, including Bruce Patman *and* Jake Hamilton, were playing touch football. Finally, she had a chance to show them the new, improved Jessica Wakefield!

"Over here!" Bruce shouted, sprinting down the field.

Jake threw the ball in a perfect arc, but it sailed over Bruce's head and landed on the sidelines just ahead of Jessica.

Jessica's heart beat faster with excitement. Now they would definitely notice her. She tried to pick up her pace.

Bruce ran over to pick up the ball. Jessica stared straight ahead and tried to look like she wasn't about to keel over from exhaustion.

"Hey, Jessica!" Bruce called out.

Jessica turned and waved.

"I didn't know it was Halloween!" Bruce said, laughing. He turned around and yelled, "Hey, guys, look at the purple alien!"

Jessica gritted her teeth. Bruce was the cutest boy in the seventh grade, but that didn't mean he couldn't be a jerk sometimes.

"What are you doing, anyway? You look like you're about to die," Bruce commented. A couple of the other boys ran over to them.

"I'm running," Jessica gasped.

"Really? It looks like you're walking," Jerry McAllister said, laughing.

"How'd you get your face to match your outfit?" Charlie Cashman joked.

Jessica didn't say anything. She just kept running as fast as she could. She hated being teased by Bruce and his friends. Once she was out of sight, Jessica slowed down to a walk. *Maybe getting into shape isn't all it's cracked up to be*, she thought, sitting down on a park bench.

Then she remembered Greg Voynow. She stood up and slowly started running again. She would show those boys. When Greg came to Sweet Valley and talked to her instead of them, they would be sorry they had laughed at her!

"How was school today?" Mr. Wakefield asked the twins Tuesday evening.

"It was OK," Elizabeth said.

"Just OK?" Mr. Wakefield asked as he passed the bowl of green beans to Steven.

"Well, we had a Unicorn meeting and we decided to throw a big party in a couple of weeks," Jessica announced.

"Whoa, how exciting!" Steven exclaimed.

Jessica glared at him. "It's going to be a costume party. And you're *not* invited."

The phone rang, and Jessica pushed her chair back from the dining room table. "That's probably Janet. I'll get it." She hurried into the kitchen.

The next thing Elizabeth heard was, "It is! Well, this is her sister, Jessica. I'm so glad you called, Greg."

Elizabeth jumped up from her chair and ran to the phone.

"I'll see you soon, I hope," Jessica said, then she handed the phone to Elizabeth. "He sounds as cute as he looks!" she whispered.

"Hello. This is Elizabeth."

"Hi, Elizabeth, this is Greg Voynow. I hope I'm not calling at a bad time, but I just got your letter and I wanted to call right away," Greg said.

"Thank you so much, Mr. Voynow," Elizabeth said.

"Please call me Greg," he said.

"OK . . . Greg," Elizabeth said uncertainly.

"I'd definitely like to help your friend," Greg went on. "I'm not sure what his specific reading problem is, but whatever it is, he needs to get some help. But I remember that I was pretty sensitive about my problem, and I don't think he'd appreciate me just walking up to him and saying, 'Hey, I hear you have a reading problem.' You know what I mean?" Greg asked.

"Yes, I do," Elizabeth replied. "You're right. That won't work. He's really sensitive, and he might not talk to you at all if he gets upset. But I think I have an idea."

"Go ahead," Greg urged her.

"Well, his name is Danny Jackson, and like I said, he's a really good runner. He's broken quite a few school and district records this year," Elizabeth said.

"You know, I think I've read about him in the newspaper," Greg said.

"You probably have. Anyway, he's been getting into a lot of trouble at school. The principal finally suspended him from the track team. I've noticed that ever since he sits and watches practice every afternoon. I was thinking that maybe you could sort of just show up at the track. Maybe you could say you heard about him or the team or something. There's a big meet coming up, and Sweet Valley was favored to win, until now," Elizabeth explained.

"And if I can get him into a conversation about track, maybe he'll tell me what's wrong," Greg said. "That might work. It's worth a try."

"I'm so glad you can help," Elizabeth said.

"I'll be glad to, if I can. How does tomorrow sound, Elizabeth? What if I come by the school around three?" Greg asked.

"That sounds great. Thanks so much," Elizabeth said. It was really going to happen! She was going to meet Greg Voynow! "Why don't I meet you outside the gym door?" she suggested. "That way we can walk over to the track together and I can show you who he is."

"I'll be there at three," Greg promised.

As Elizabeth hung up the phone, she noticed that her hands were shaking. She didn't know what she was more nervous about: Greg talking to Danny—or Greg talking to her!

"So what did he say?" Jessica asked, tapping her foot impatiently.

"*Shh*," Elizabeth whispered to her sister. "Let's talk about this upstairs after dinner."

*   *   *

When they got upstairs, Jessica hurled herself onto her sister's bed. "Ouch."

"What's wrong?" Elizabeth asked.

"I'm just a little sore from exercising. So what did he say?" Jessica persisted.

Elizabeth sat down next to Jessica. "He's going to do it, Jess. He's coming to school tomorrow!" she said excitedly.

"That's great! What time?" Jessica asked.

"Three o'clock. I don't think I'm going to be able to sleep tonight. I'm so nervous."

"So where should I meet up with you?" Jessica asked.

Elizabeth was confused. "Did you think you were going to meet Greg, too?"

"I found the article about him, didn't I?" Jessica pointed out.

"Sure, but . . ." Elizabeth didn't want to admit it, but she didn't want to share Greg with anybody. She was looking forward to getting a chance to talk to him, and she knew that if Jessica was there, she wouldn't get a word in edgewise. "Look, Jessica," she said, "Greg's coming to Sweet Valley to see Danny, not us."

"I know that! I just think I should be able to at least say hello to him," Jessica said.

"I'm sorry, Jessica. I told Greg I'd meet him alone," Elizabeth said firmly.

"It's not fair, Lizzie," Jessica said. "If I hadn't found that article, you wouldn't even know that Greg existed."

"I really am sorry, Jess," Elizabeth replied.

"Fine," Jessica said angrily. She stood up and stomped back to her bedroom.

But Elizabeth had a feeling her sister wasn't going to give up that easily.

Twelve

◇

"What am I going to wear?" Elizabeth wailed the next morning. It wasn't like her to spend half an hour getting dressed. Jessica was the one who usually worried about having the perfect outfit.

Jessica peered into her sister's room. "Do you want my advice?" she asked.

"Please," Elizabeth begged her.

"Wear the blue and white sweater. It brings out the color of your eyes." Jessica stepped in front of Elizabeth and examined her own reflection in the mirror. She was wearing a denim miniskirt and a pink T-shirt.

"You look great," Elizabeth told her.

Jessica moved closer to the mirror and ran her fingers through her hair. "I'd look a lot better if I had earrings to match this shirt."

"It won't be too long," Elizabeth said, slipping the sweater over her head.

"Two years isn't long? Elizabeth, have you

lost your mind? Lila's getting her ears pierced *this* weekend, and I still have to wait a lifetime!"

Elizabeth noticed that Jessica was taking more time than usual to get ready, too. "You're not still thinking of trying to meet Greg, are you?" she asked.

Jessica put on some lip gloss. "No. I just want to look good in case he happens to walk around the school. He might, you know."

Elizabeth shrugged her shoulders. "I guess so."

"I want to make sure I'm ready, just in case," Jessica said.

"Oh, OK." Elizabeth couldn't blame her for that. Now if only she could figure out what she was going to say to Greg when she saw him!

It was finally a quarter to three. Elizabeth had been counting the minutes all day long. She quickened her pace as she walked down the hall toward her locker.

"Elizabeth!" someone called behind her.

Elizabeth turned and saw Mr. Bowman hurrying toward her, his bright green tie flipping over his shoulder. "Elizabeth, there's an emergency. We seem to have lost all the copies of tomorrow's *Sixers*," he said.

"It's OK, we'll run off a new batch now," Elizabeth said. Then she turned and ran down the hall to Jessica's locker.

Jessica was slipping into her jean jacket, and she smiled when she saw her sister. "Hi, Liz. Are you nervous about meeting Mr. Superstar?"

"Yes," Elizabeth said quickly, "but I have a big problem right now, and I need your help."

"What is it, Lizzie?" Jessica asked, looking concerned.

Elizabeth sighed in frustration. "There's a problem with tomorrow's *Sixers* edition. The copies we made yesterday are missing, and Mr. Bowman asked me to run off some more. But I can't because I have to meet Greg in ten minutes."

"Is that all? Get someone else to make the copies," Jessica said.

"Could you do it?" Elizabeth asked. "Please?"

"Me?" Jessica looked shocked. "I don't work on the *Sixers*!"

"Jess, please, I really need you to do this for me," Elizabeth pleaded.

"Lizzie, you know I'm not good at running that machine. I have a better idea. Why don't I go meet Greg for you?" Jessica suggested.

Elizabeth frowned. That wasn't what she had in mind at all. "I don't know," she said.

"Look, why don't you go start making the copies? How long can it take?" Jessica said. "When you're done, come outside. I'll stall Greg so that he can meet you before he goes off and talks to Danny. You'll still get to see him."

"I guess that's the only thing I can do," Elizabeth said with a sigh. "I'd better hurry. See you in a few minutes!"

Jessica flipped her hair over her shoulder and tried to look casual as she walked over to

Greg. He was even better-looking than he appeared in the magazine. He was about six feet tall with wavy blond hair and bright blue eyes. He was wearing jeans, a college sweatshirt, and running shoes.

"Hello," Jessica said, giving him one of her best smiles. "I'm Jessica Wakefield."

Greg held out his hand, and Jessica shook it. "Greg Voynow. Nice to meet you."

"Same here," Jessica said.

"You're Elizabeth's sister, aren't you?" Greg asked.

Jessica nodded.

"Is she coming?" Greg asked.

"Oh, uh, actually, she got tied up with a school project, so she asked me to meet you instead," Jessica replied.

"That's too bad. I was really looking forward to meeting her," Greg said.

Jessica decided to change the subject. "It's a real thrill to meet you!" she said enthusiastically. "I'm a runner, too, and I really admire what you've done."

"Oh, are you on the track team?" Greg asked her.

"Not yet," Jessica said. "You know, it's funny that I'm meeting you today, because actually, *I* was the one who found the article about you in *Sports Today*," she told him. "When I read about you, I told Elizabeth, Greg has so much in common with Danny, you know, maybe they should meet each other."

"Well, that's great," Greg said. "Listen, Elizabeth was going to show me where her friend was sitting, so I could go talk to him." Greg shielded his eyes from the sun and looked over at the bleachers in front of the track. "There's someone sitting over there now. Is that him?"

"Hmm, let me see." Jessica had meant what she said when she'd told Elizabeth she was going to stall Greg—especially since it meant she could spend more time with him. "I can't tell from here. Maybe we should go a little closer."

She and Greg slowly approached the bleachers. "Well?" Greg asked. "Is that Danny?"

Why couldn't Danny have gotten a detention today or something? Jessica thought. She nodded. "It sure is." She wished she could think of something else to say to hold Greg's attention.

"Thanks a lot, Jessica," Greg said. "Tell Elizabeth I'm sorry I didn't get to see her. Maybe next time." He smiled at Jessica, and then started walking over to Danny.

Next time, Jessica thought with a smile. *There's going to be a next time? I can't wait to tell Lila about this!*

"Hi. Aren't you Danny Jackson?"

"Yeah," Danny said without looking up.

"I'm Greg Voynow."

Danny jerked to attention. He stared up at Greg for a minute without saying anything. "Wow, I can't believe it," he finally said. "You really *are* Greg Voynow!"

"The one and only," Greg said as he sat down next to Danny.

"What are you doing *here*?" Danny asked. "And how come you knew my name?"

"Well, I don't live too far from here, and I read in the paper a couple of weeks ago about how well your team was doing. So I thought I'd come out here and check you guys out. See how good you really are," Greg said. "I recognized you from your picture in the paper. You're quite a runner."

"Oh." Danny nodded. "Thanks." It was just his luck. One of the biggest track stars in the world had come to Sweet Valley, and there he was, sitting in the bleachers!

"So why aren't you out there?" Greg motioned toward the track with his thumb. The rest of the team was doing their warm-up laps.

"I, uh, got injured," Danny lied.

"That's too bad. What's the problem?" Greg asked.

"I pulled my hamstring," Danny said, naming an injury he had heard a lot about on television. He rubbed his leg.

"That's happened to me a few times," Greg said. "But don't worry. It'll go away if you rest for a few days. Well, since I can't watch you run, what do you say we go get some ice cream? My treat."

"Don't you want to watch the rest of the team?" Danny asked. "We have some other good runners, like my friend Jim."

"No, I really came to see you. You're the one with the district record, and I think we should celebrate that. Let's go find the biggest hot fudge sundae in Sweet Valley. That's how I celebrate all my victories," Greg told him. "Besides, ice cream is good for pulled hamstrings. Old family remedy."

"OK," Danny agreed, laughing.

"I've got my car, so name the place," Greg said as they walked down the bleachers.

Danny couldn't believe Greg was being so friendly to him. He noticed the rest of the team staring as they walked off toward the parking lot. He pretended he had a slight limp. "Casey's Place at the mall is the best," he told Greg.

"Casey's it is," Greg said. "Hop in!"

The waitress placed a supersize butterscotch sundae in front of Danny and a hot fudge in front of Greg. "This is huge!" Greg said. "I like this place."

Danny picked up his spoon and dug into the sundae. He had been having such a good time with Greg, he hadn't even noticed how hungry he was.

"So how's everything else at school?" Greg asked. "Are you in any clubs?"

Danny shook his head. "I'm not really into that stuff."

"Well, what's your favorite subject?"

Danny shrugged. "I don't really have one."

"I know what you mean. I was the same way when I was in school," Greg said, wiping his mouth with a napkin. "I couldn't wait to get outside and run after school, so I spent most of my time *in* school waiting to get out. That was a huge mistake."

"What do you mean?" Danny asked. "You made it to the Olympics. You probably wouldn't have if you didn't concentrate so hard on running."

"Well, I almost *didn't* make it," Greg said. "See, my high school teachers always passed me to the next grade no matter what, because I was such a good athlete. I did OK in some subjects, but in others I was really behind. Then I won an athletic scholarship to college. That was great, but I ended up failing three out of four classes my first semester, and I lost my scholarship. And do you know why I failed, Danny? Because I had never learned how to read."

Danny clenched his spoon tighter. He felt his whole body tense up. "Is that why you're here?" he asked Greg slowly. "To give me a lecture?"

"No," Greg said. "I'm here to talk to you about your reading problem."

"Well, maybe I don't want to talk about it!" Danny said angrily. "And how do you know about it, anyway?" Elizabeth Wakefield's name flashed through his head. Could she have gotten in touch with Greg Voynow?

"That doesn't matter," Greg said. "Listen, I

just wanted to tell you what happened to me so that it doesn't happen to you. It wasn't until I was nineteen that I could admit I had a learning disability. I wasted a lot of years. Admitting I had a problem was the hardest thing I ever had to do. But once I did, I got help for it, and it didn't take me too long to learn how to read after that. Eventually I went back to college, and you know the rest."

Danny stared into his sundae, mashing the ice cream with his spoon. He wasn't sure whether to believe Greg or not. How could a world-famous track star have the same problem he did? *Maybe it's not such a strange thing*, Danny said to himself. *Maybe lots of other people have the same problem.*

He glanced up at Greg. Maybe he knew a way Danny could learn to read without telling the whole world he was stupid.

"Well?" Greg said after a minute or two.

"You're right," Danny finally admitted. "I can't read. Well, I can read a little, but there are a lot of words I don't know. And I'm not injured. I'm not on the track team anymore because the principal kicked me off."

"Because you couldn't read?" Greg asked.

"No. Because I goof around every time the teachers ask me to read," Danny explained. It felt good to be telling someone the truth for once.

"I hid my problem from my teachers a lot of the time, too—for as long as I could get away with it. And I didn't tell my parents," Greg said. "I was afraid they'd get mad."

"So am I," Danny said. "My parents are very smart. I know they're going to be disappointed in me when they find out I'm not."

"Danny, having a learning disability doesn't mean you're not smart," Greg said. "You do well in some subjects, don't you?"

"Yeah, I guess so," Danny said.

"Lots of smart kids have trouble reading," Greg said. "Believe me, you're not the only one. All you have to do is tell someone about it."

"Like who?" Danny asked. He was dreading telling his parents and his teachers. He had been dreading it for years.

"Your guidance counselor, or the principal, or any teacher you want to," Greg said. "Promise me you'll do it. And not next week or next year. Tomorrow."

Danny groaned. But he liked Mr. Bowman. Maybe he could talk to him. "All right," Danny said. "I'll do it."

"Think of it this way. The sooner you get it over with, the sooner you'll be back on that track!" Greg said. "Now, it looks to me like you need another sundae."

Danny looked down at his dish and laughed. It was a giant pool of melted ice cream. "Thanks," he said.

Elizabeth dumped some more mimeographing fluid into the machine. She felt as if she had been trapped in the office forever. The mimeograph machine wasn't working properly. She started turning the handle and the first few copies came out fine. Then, suddenly, the machine started ripping the paper into shreds instead of printing on it.

"I'll never finish this!" Elizabeth cried out in frustration.

"Is something wrong, Elizabeth?" Mr. Bowman asked, walking into the room.

"Oh, I'm so glad to see you!" Elizabeth exclaimed. "This machine is acting up."

"Well, I found the other copies, so it doesn't matter," Mr. Bowman said. "It turns out that someone had moved them and forgot to tell me about it. I'm sorry you had to waste your time, Elizabeth."

"That's OK," Elizabeth said. "I have to run. See you later!" She grabbed her backpack off the table and bolted out the door. She couldn't wait to meet Greg. She hoped she hadn't gotten any purple marks on her face while she was working on the ditto machine.

But when she ran out the door by the gym, Jessica and Greg were nowhere in sight. *I wonder where they went*, Elizabeth thought.

She saw a cluster of people standing by the track and decided to ask them if they knew where Jessica had gone. But when she approached them, she saw her sister surrounded by the boys on the track team.

"I can't believe Greg Voynow was here, at our school," Jim Sturbridge was saying.

"He must have read about Danny's new records in the L.A. newspaper," Jim said. "My father said Danny was written up a few weeks ago."

"It's too bad Danny's not on the team anymore," Colin Harmon said.

"Jessica? What happened?" Elizabeth asked.

"Greg Voynow was here! You know, the track star," Jessica said innocently. She had promised Elizabeth she wouldn't tell anyone about the plan to help Danny. "And I got to talk to him!" she added excitedly.

"It's too bad I missed him," Elizabeth said with a pointed look at her sister.

Jessica stepped away from the crowd, and she and Elizabeth walked off. "I'm sorry, Liz. He was kind of in a hurry," Jessica said. "He and Danny left a while ago, so it looks like our plan is working."

Our *plan?* Elizabeth thought. "Do you know where they went?" she asked.

"No. I tried to stay out of the way, so Danny wouldn't get suspicious. Lizzie, you wouldn't believe how good-looking Greg is in person!" Jessica said dreamily. "His hair is long now, and it's got these little curls at the end of it. And he's taller than I thought he would be, too. He was *so* nice. It's really too bad you didn't see him."

"Yes, it is," Elizabeth agreed. "Maybe I'll get another chance soon." She was disappointed that she missed him, but she was glad Greg was talking to Danny. After all, getting help for Danny was the most important thing.

"I hope you do, Lizzie," Jessica said. "But I'm glad I saw him today. Did I tell you about his eyes?"

Elizabeth couldn't help smiling. Sometimes Jessica was really too much!

Thirteen

◇

"Earth to Elizabeth," Amy said. "Come in, please."

Elizabeth looked at Amy and smiled sheepishly. "Sorry."

"What's going on? You've been daydreaming all day," Amy said.

"Did you hear about the track star that was here yesterday after school?" Elizabeth said. She couldn't tell Amy the whole truth, but she could tell her what was bothering her.

"Greg something or other, right? Yeah, I heard he was here watching the track team," Amy said.

"I just wish I could have met him," Elizabeth said. "He's really incredible."

"Jessica got to meet him, didn't she? I heard her telling a bunch of people about it. She said she talked to him for a long time, and he was really cute and nice," Amy said. "Then I heard he and Danny went off somewhere together. I wonder where they were going?"

Elizabeth shrugged. "Beats me."

As they walked past Mr. Clark's office, the door opened and Mr. Bowman stepped out, followed by Danny.

"What do you think that was about?" Elizabeth whispered.

"Nothing unusual, if you ask me," Amy replied. "He's always in Mr. Clark's office."

Elizabeth knew that was true, but she was sure this time was different. For one thing, Danny was actually smiling as he left the principal's office. And Mr. Bowman didn't look angry either. That had to mean something good!

"What was he wearing?" Janet Howell asked.

"He had on jeans, and a big college sweat shirt. He looked adorable," Jessica said. She took her sandwich out of her lunch bag and took a large bite. Exercising made her extremely hungry.

"How old is he?" Grace Oliver wanted to know.

"Twenty-five, I think." Jessica took a sip of milk. "But he seems a lot younger."

"I still don't understand why he was here," Lila said.

"I told you, he came to watch the track team," Jessica explained.

"I didn't know they were doing *that* well," Lila said.

"They're undefeated, aren't they? And Danny Jackson set some new records a few weeks ago. It was in the newspaper and Greg read about it, that's all," Jessica said casually. She had promised Elizabeth she would keep Danny's problem a secret, and she wasn't going to let her twin down. Besides, Jessica almost felt sorry for her sister. Elizabeth had really wanted to meet Greg. "I just happened to be in the right place at the right time," Jessica told the other girls.

"I'll say!" Janet shook her head. "What did you talk about?"

"Well, I told him about how I was working out and everything," Jessica said.

"Did you get his autograph?" Grace asked.

"No, it all happened so fast, I didn't have time to," Jessica said.

"I thought you said you talked to him for twenty minutes," Lila commented.

"Well, what I mean is, I got so wrapped up in our conversation that I forgot to," Jessica hurried to explain. "If you saw him, you'd understand why."

"Good afternoon." Mr. Bowman smiled at his class. "When class ended yesterday, we were discussing—"

Just then the door opened and a man carrying a briefcase walked into the classroom. "Excuse me," he said. "I hope I'm not interrupting."

"We were just getting started," Mr. Bowman said. "Can I help you?"

The man approached Mr. Bowman, and the two started talking quietly. Then Mr. Bowman turned around and faced the class. "Danny, will you come here for a minute?" he said.

Danny walked to the front of the room, and the other man spoke to him briefly. Then Danny went to his seat and collected his books.

"Danny will be missing some of our classes over the next several weeks," Mr. Bowman announced. He smiled at Danny and said, "Good luck."

"Thanks," Danny said. "I'll need it."

"No, you won't," Mr. Bowman assured him. "You'll do fine."

Everyone in the class watched Danny leave with the man. Jessica thought furiously. Did this have something to do with Danny's conversation with Greg the day before? *That's it! He must have a tutor now, to teach him how to read,* Jessica told herself. She decided to talk to Elizabeth about it as soon as class was over.

At last the bell rang. Jessica grabbed her books and signalled to her twin to meet in the hallway.

"That definitely was a tutor, don't you think?" Jessica asked when Elizabeth appeared.

"Maybe," Elizabeth said.

"Hey, Elizabeth! Great article!" Jim Sturbridge waved the latest issue of the *Sixers* in the air. He was walking down the hall toward them.

"Thanks," Elizabeth replied.

"Did you hear the good news?" Jim asked the twins. "Danny's back on the team!"

"You're kidding!" Elizabeth exclaimed.

"Nope. Mr. Clark gave him the OK today. Now we're going to walk all over the other teams for sure," Jim said excitedly. "Hey, Colin!" he yelled down the hall. "Wait up! See you later," he said to Jessica and Elizabeth. Then he ran off down the hall.

"Do you know what this means?" Elizabeth said softly. "Danny must have told Mr. Clark the truth about not being able to read."

"I'm not surprised," Jessica said.

Elizabeth looked at her. "Why not?"

"Greg can do anything," Jessica said confidently. "You should have seen him, Lizzie."

Elizabeth groaned. She didn't want to hear any more about her sister's meeting with the track star. "I'm going to the library, Jess. I'll see you later, OK?"

"What are you doing?" Steven asked. "Yoga?"

"For your information, I'm stretching my muscles," Jessica said.

"What muscles?" Steven asked. "I don't see any."

Jessica gave her brother a dirty look.

"Sor-ry!" Steven turned and walked out of the living room.

Jessica ran up to her room to get her sweat shirt. She was going to jog down to the beach and back. It was a long way, but she felt ready. She was pulling the sweat shirt on over her head when the phone rang.

"Jessica! It's for you!" Mrs. Wakefield called up the stairs.

Jessica hurried down to the kitchen and took the phone from her mother. "Hello?"

"Jessica! Guess what?" Lila cried.

"You got your ears pierced," Jessica answered quietly.

"You should see them. They look great!" Lila said.

"Did it hurt?" Jessica asked.

"Not really. Maybe a little. But it was worth it!" Lila declared.

"I bet. Well, I have to go, Lila. I'm jogging down to the beach," Jessica said.

"You're kidding! Why don't you take the bus?" Lila demanded.

"Because I'm doing it to get exercise, silly," Jessica said impatiently.

"Oh. Well, have fun! I'm going to try on all my jewelry and see how it looks with my earrings," Lila said. "Call me later!"

"OK," Jessica agreed, even though she was tired of listening to Lila brag. " 'Bye."

Jessica collapsed onto the sand and stretched her arms over her head. She felt exhausted. She pulled off her sweat shirt and made a pillow out of it. Then she lay down and closed her eyes. The sun felt wonderful.

When she got up a while later and started walking down the beach, she noticed her right foot really hurt. She stopped and took off her sneaker to look at it.

"Oh, no!" Jessica cried when she pulled off her sock. A blister the size of a quarter was on the back of her heel.

Bruce Patman and his friends were just getting out of a car when they noticed Jessica limping up the beach.

"Hey, I think she's hurt," Jake Hamilton said. He walked over to her. "Are you OK?"

"I'm fine," Jessica said miserably. "I just have a blister, that's all."

"Do you want a ride home? My mom could take you," Jake offered.

"Well, if it's not too much trouble." Jessica shrugged. "Sure."

Jake ran over to the car and spoke to his mother. A few seconds later, she pulled up in front of Jessica. "Hop in," she said with a smile.

"Thank you, Mrs. Hamilton. Thanks, Jake," Jessica called to him as she climbed into the car.

"What happened to you?" Mrs. Wakefield asked when Jessica came through the door.

"I got a blister," Jessica said.

"Let me see it," Mrs. Wakefield said.

Jessica pulled off her sock and her mother examined the blister. "This looks very painful, honey. Why don't you go upstairs and soak in a hot bath for a while?"

"Good idea," Jessica said as she crawled up the stairs. But before she got into the tub, she decided to weigh herself.

"That can't be right!" she screamed. She stepped off the scale, and then back on. The reading was three pounds more than she had weighed *before* she started working out!

She thought about how much time she had spent exercising. She had missed two Unicorn meetings and a Boosters practice. And what were the results? She had an enormous blister, she was exhausted, and she had *gained* weight. And on top of all that, she had been humiliated twice in front of Bruce and Jake. The only time Jake had been nice to her was when she was hurt!

Jessica walked into her room and picked up the exercise magazine from her bed. "What do you know, anyway?" she said, dropping it into her trash can.

Fourteen

◇

Elizabeth watched Danny walk into English class and take his usual seat in the back. It had been nearly a week since his meeting with Greg. Whatever Greg said had obviously worked, because Danny hadn't acted up once in any of his classes. The district track meet was that Thursday. Everyone said Danny was running better than ever.

These days, Danny's schedule in English class varied. Sometimes he stayed for half a class and sometimes he skipped the whole thing. Elizabeth had heard that Danny had skipped a few track practices as well.

About fifteen minutes into class, Mr. Bowman stopped and said, "Danny? It's quarter past."

Before Danny left, he walked over to Mr. Bowman and whispered something to him. Mr. Bowman nodded. "I will," he said. "See you tomorrow." He watched Danny walk out the door, then he turned back to the class.

"Danny wanted me to explain something to you," Mr. Bowman began. "The reason he's leaving class is because he needs a tutor to help him catch up on his reading skills. Danny has a reading disability that is called dyslexia. Perhaps you've heard of it before. What it means is, he can't see some words right, because his brain reverses the letters. For example, the word *saw* might look like *was* to him.

"Dyslexia is fairly common," Mr. Bowman continued. "It's usually detected at an earlier age, but unfortunately, none of Danny's teachers at his old school recognized the symptoms. I'm sure that with careful tutoring and some hard work on Danny's part, he'll soon be reading on a higher level. One more thing: having a learning disability does not mean Danny is any less intelligent than anyone else in this room. Both Thomas Edison and Albert Einstein had difficulty in school when they were children—and as you know, it didn't stop them from being geniuses later in life! Now, does anyone have any questions?"

"How did he get it?" Belinda Layton asked.

"It's not something you get, like a cold," Mr. Bowman explained. "Sometimes it's inherited from your parents, sometimes it isn't."

"How come Danny is so good at math?" Jessica asked. "Doesn't he mix the numbers around, too?"

"Apparently not," Mr. Bowman said, "although some dyslexics have trouble with arithmetic, too. Now, before we move on to the story we'll be reading today, I'd like to make one final comment. I don't want anyone to make a big deal about this, or to treat Danny any differently. Is that understood?''

There was a murmur of yeses around the room.

"Good," Mr. Bowman said. "Now let's get back to our story."

Thursday afternoon, it was standing room only at the Sweet Valley Middle School track. Five other schools were competing in the district meet. Parents filled the stands, along with teachers, classmates, and friends. The Boosters were standing in front of the bleachers, leading the crowd in a cheer.

Elizabeth and Julie managed to get through the crowd so that they were standing near the finish line. The 400-meter race, the last and most important event of the meet, was about to begin. Danny held both the school and the district records for the event. Sweet Valley was winning the meet, but only by a few points. Now it was up to Danny to make sure Sweet Valley won the district championship.

"I can't believe we made it through that crowd." Julie looked up and down the track. "We have the *best* view!"

"Good, because the race is about to start," Elizabeth said. She watched as the Sweet Valley team gathered in a huddle.

"I thought only football players did that," Julie observed.

"They must be getting Danny psyched. Coach Stern's probably giving him a big last-minute pep talk," Elizabeth said.

The team let out a loud yell, and then one of the judges announced that the 400-meter race would be next. Elizabeth watched as Danny jogged around the inside of the track, warming up. He looked nervous, but confident, too. He had already won the 800 meter earlier in the afternoon.

The judge called out the names of the participants, who lined up in their lanes. Then the judge called out, "On your marks . . . get set . . . GO!"

Danny took the lead immediately. Elizabeth stood on her tiptoes to get a glimpse of him as he sped around the first corner. When the runners came out of the turn and headed down the backstretch, Danny pulled out in front by a good ten yards.

The noise from the bleachers was deafening. Everyone was standing on their feet, yelling, "Go, Danny!" The track team joined in a chant of "Dan-ny, Dan-ny, Dan-ny!"

Danny came around the last corner at top speed, taking long strides. The other runners didn't have a chance of beating him. He cruised through the tape at the finish line with a big grin on his face.

"All right, Danny!" Elizabeth yelled.

"Way to go!" Julie called as he jogged past them on the track.

"It's a new state record!" Coach Stern shouted, holding his stopwatch over his head.

Jim raised his fists in the air. "We won! We won!" he yelled. He ran over to Danny and threw his arm around his shoulders. The rest of the team rushed over and surrounded Danny, shouting their congratulations.

Elizabeth looked at the stands. They seemed to be shaking from all the stomping and cheering. When she turned back to the track, Danny was talking to a man and a woman, both dressed in business suits, who Elizabeth recognized as his parents. They were both smiling.

Elizabeth grinned. She thought it was wonderful that his parents were showing him some support. It might have been the first track meet they had attended, but Elizabeth doubted it would be their last. And they had certainly chosen a good one to come to!

A crackle came over the public address system. "Ladies and gentlemen, the winner of the District Seventeen middle school track meet is . . . Sweet Valley Middle School!" one of the judges announced.

Another loud cheer went up from the bleachers and the track.

"Their team's score will go down in the record books, folks, because it's the best one in thirty years," the judge went on. "Second place goes to Pinecrest, with an impressive showing, and third place goes to Big Mesa Middle School. One last announcement. Daniel Jackson of Sweet Valley has just set a state record in the four-hundred meter race. Congratulations, Daniel!''

The crowd roared for Danny.

"Thank you all for coming and showing your support for these fine athletes," the announcer said. "It's been a great afternoon!"

Elizabeth agreed. It had been a great afternoon—and a great week.

"All right, everyone," Mrs. Arnette said. "Please walk quietly down the hall to the auditorium. No running. Not even you, Danny." She smiled.

"Can you believe that? That's the first time I ever heard Mrs. Arnette make a joke," Lila said as she stood up.

"I told you Danny would have a good effect on our classes," Jessica said. "I'm so glad we're having an assembly today." The principal had decided to hold a special assembly on Friday to honor the track team, so they were getting out of class early.

Elizabeth smiled as she walked down the hall beside her twin. "Because you like social studies so much?" she teased Jessica.

Jessica grinned. "Besides, when we have all-school assemblies, it's a good opportunity to check out the crowd. Right, Lila?"

"It sure is," Lila said. She was walking in front of them. "But it's important to get a good seat. You know, one in the back, so you can see everyone," she said.

"I think you two have boy-watching down to a science," Elizabeth commented. As she walked into the auditorium, she spotted Amy sitting in one of the back rows. Amy waved at her. "I'm going to sit with Amy," she told Jessica. "Is that far enough back for you?"

Jessica surveyed the room. A row of seventh-grade boys were sitting just in front of Amy. "Looks fine to me," Jessica said happily.

Elizabeth edged her way along the row and sat down next to her friend. "Hi," she said. Jessica sat next to Elizabeth, with Lila on the end. Jessica and Lila started whispering immediately.

Mr. Clark tapped his finger against the microphone. "Good morning," he greeted the crowd. "We're here today to honor fifteen very special people." He turned around and gestured at the boys sitting behind him on the stage. "Stand up, boys. I'd like to introduce the new district champions, our very own track team!"

Mr. Clark named each member of the team, and everyone in the audience clapped.

"And now, I'd like to present a special award," Mr. Clark said. "For the teammate who did the most for his team, the boy who put Sweet Valley Middle School on the map by setting a new state record yesterday . . . Danny Jackson!"

The crowd cheered enthusiastically as Mr.

Clark handed Danny a plaque in recognition of his achievements. Danny shook Mr. Clark's hand and sat back down. He was blushing from all the attention, but he looked happy.

"I'm glad that Danny is only in the sixth grade," Mr. Clark said, "because I'm going to enjoy watching him break even more records over the next couple of years. Now I'd like to introduce today's special guest, who is someone who has been setting records for the past several years. His most recent accomplishment was setting a new world record in the four-hundred-meter hurdles. Boys and girls, would you please give a warm welcome to Mr. Greg Voynow."

Everyone clapped enthusiastically as Greg walked out from the side of the stage and up to the microphone.

Jessica squeezed Elizabeth's arm. "I told you he was better-looking in person," she whispered excitedly.

Elizabeth was speechless. She nodded in agreement.

"Hello, everyone," Greg said, smiling at the audience. "I'm here today for two reasons. First, to congratulate the team on all their hard work. I know how tough it is to train every day, and I admire their dedication." Greg paused for a moment.

"The second thing I want to talk to you about is another kind of dedication, the dedication it requires to get a good education. It's very important to stay in school and learn everything you can. As some of you may know, I was not the best student when I was in school," Greg said.

As Greg told the assembly about his learning disability, Elizabeth gazed up at him. Greg was here, in person! *This time I'm going to make sure I meet him*, Elizabeth decided.

"It took me a few years of tutoring to learn how to read, but I got the hang of it," Greg was saying. "I went back to college, our team won the national championships, and after that I went to the Olympics."

Several people in the audience started cheering and applauding Greg.

He held up his hand. "I'm not telling you this for applause. I'm here because I want to tell you that if you do have any kind of problem in school, you shouldn't hide it. Tell your teacher or your counselor or your parents about it. They can help you. But no one can help you if you won't admit you're having trouble. It takes guts to face up to your problems, but I've met a lot of kids with learning disabilities, and they've all been a lot happier once they did." He turned and smiled at Danny.

Danny smiled back at him.

"There's someone in the audience who deserves special recognition," Greg went on. "Now, this person is not on the track team, but in my opinion she's a real champion. She's the one who got in touch with me when she recognized that one of her fellow students was deeply troubled. I did some of the work, but she deserves all of the credit."

Jessica sat up straighter in her chair. She was confident that Greg would call her name.

"Elizabeth Wakefield, will you please come up here?" Greg said, a big grin on his face.

"Elizabeth, you didn't tell me about this!" Amy said.

Elizabeth was so surprised she couldn't move.

"Get up," Amy urged her. She pulled Elizabeth's arm off the seat and pushed her to her feet. "Go on, everyone's waiting!"

Somehow, Elizabeth made her way out to the aisle and walked toward the stage. When she stepped up onto the stage, Greg walked up to her, leaned down—and kissed her on the cheek!

Mr. Clark stepped up to the podium. "Once again, thanks for a great season, boys! And thank you, Greg, for sharing your story with us. This assembly is dismissed."

Total pandemonium broke out in the auditorium as kids rushed to the doors.

"Looks like things haven't changed since I was in school," Greg remarked as he and Elizabeth walked off the stage.

Elizabeth laughed.

"Elizabeth, I really appreciate everything you did for Danny," Greg said. "I know he does, too."

"Thanks," Elizabeth said. "But you're the one who really made the difference."

"Let's look at it this way," Greg said with a grin. "We make a good team."

Elizabeth smiled. This was going to go on record as one of her all-time-best days!

"So what did it *feel* like when he kissed you?" Julie asked at lunch.

"I don't even remember," Elizabeth said. "I was too surprised."

"Why didn't you tell us what you were up to?" Amy asked.

"I couldn't. Danny made me promise I wouldn't tell anyone when I found out he couldn't read," Elizabeth explained.

"I don't know if I could have kept a secret for that long," Amy admitted.

"Well, actually, I did tell Jessica about it," Elizabeth said.

"And *she* kept it a secret?" Julie said.

Elizabeth nodded. "Sure. Jess can be pretty responsible, you know."

"Look, they're bringing out a big cake!" Amy cried.

"Let's get some," Julie said, jumping up from her chair. "Come on, Elizabeth."

They rushed up to the table at the side of the lunchroom, where a cafeteria worker was setting down a huge sheet cake. It had chocolate frosting on it shaped in a dark-chocolate oval, representing the track. In white writing it said, "Congratulations, Sweet Valley Track!" Kids crowded around on all sides as the cake was cut, put on plates, and handed to them.

While she was waiting for her piece, Elizabeth felt someone tap her on the shoulder. She turned around and saw Danny standing behind her. "Hi," she said in a friendly tone. They hadn't spoken to each other since the day Danny had gotten so mad at her in the library.

"Hi," he said. "I, uh, I just wanted to say thanks."

Elizabeth smiled. "You're welcome."

"Sorry about throwing the book and stuff," Danny said.

"It's OK. It all worked out in the end," Elizabeth said.

"Yeah, it sure did!" Danny replied with a big grin.

Elizabeth handed a piece of cake to Danny. "You should be very proud." she said.

"I can't believe Elizabeth got a kiss from that guy," Lila said. "He's gorgeous!"

"Do you think he's still here?" Ellen Riteman glanced around the cafeteria.

"I hope so," Janet said. "Boy, you were right, Jessica, He's terrific-looking! Elizabeth is so lucky."

Jessica was annoyed. Everyone was making such a big deal about Elizabeth and Greg that they had forgotten she was the one who had talked to him first.

"I still can't get over how good your earrings look, Lila," Grace Oliver said.

"Only five more weeks and I can wear anything I want," Lila said. "Jessica, when are you getting yours pierced? Your parents said it was OK, right?"

"Not exactly," Jessica mumbled.

"I told you they'd say no!" Lila told her cousin. "Jessica's parents don't let her do *any*thing."

"That's not true," Jessica argued. "They just want me to wait."

"Until you're in college, right?" Lila joked.

"No, high school," Jessica said without thinking.

"What? You have to wait until high school?" Janet stared at Jessica in disbelief.

"I have to wait until I'm fourteen," Jessica admitted.

"That's too bad," Grace said sympathetically.

"It's too bad your parents still treat you like a baby," Lila added. "You're going to be the last person in our class to get pierced ears."

Jessica fiddled with the fork on her cake plate.

"Maybe you can get some clip-ons," Janet suggested, giggling.

"Yeah, maybe I can borrow some from my grandmother for you!" Lila shrieked with laughter.

Jessica threw down her napkin and stood

up. She didn't want to listen to their teasing any longer. Somehow, she would have to find a way to change her parents' minds.

"Jess, why aren't you speaking to me?" Elizabeth asked her twin. They were walking home together after school. Jessica hadn't said one word to Elizabeth since the assembly that morning.

Jessica didn't say anything. She held her chin up and continued walking.

Elizabeth sighed. "OK, have it your way," she said. "But I'm still going to talk to you. So what are you going to do this weekend? I think I'll go to the mall and see if I can find a new pair of jeans. I'm not sure what else I'll get. Mom said I could have fifty dollars for new clothes."

"She *did*?" Jessica stopped walking.

"No, not really." Elizabeth laughed. "I just wanted to get you to open your mouth."

"Well, I don't think it's very funny," Jessica said. "And I don't think you getting all the credit from Greg in front of the whole school is funny either. I found the article about him, after all."

"Is that why you're mad at me?" Elizabeth asked. "Jess, I didn't know he was coming to the assembly today . . . and the last thing I expected was for him to call me up to the stage."

Jessica frowned. "Maybe not, but I still don't think it's fair."

"Well, I didn't think it was fair when you

got to meet Greg and I didn't. I had to listen to you telling everyone in school how thrilling it was and how he spent twenty minutes talking to you," Elizabeth said. "So now we're even."

Jessica thought about it for a minute. "I guess," she admitted. "But *I* didn't get a kiss."

"Do you want me to tell you about it?" Elizabeth asked, doing her best to imitate the mushy voice Jessica used whenever she was talking about a boy she liked.

"Oh, *Lizzie*," Jessica said in exasperation. But she smiled.

"I have good news!" Mrs. Wakefield said Saturday morning when the twins came down to breakfast. "I just spoke with Grandma and Grandpa Robertson, and they're coming to visit."

"That's nice," Jessica said as she poured herself a glass of orange juice.

"For how long?" Elizabeth asked.

"Just a few days," Mrs. Wakefield said. "Jessica, I'd like them to stay in your room, so would you mind moving back in with Elizabeth for a few days?"

Elizabeth and Jessica had shared a room up until that year, so they were used to being roommates.

"Sure," Jessica said. "It'll be fun."

"Good," Mrs. Wakefield said. "Elizabeth, you don't mind, do you?"

"Well, I'll never be able to find anything

again, but other than that it's fine with me."
She smiled at Jessica. "Just kidding, Jess."

"I'm really excited that Grandma and Grandpa
are coming," Elizabeth told Jessica after their
mother had left the room.

"Me, too," Jessica said with a grin. "They
always bring the best presents!"

*What will happen when the twins' grandparents
visit? Find out in Sweet Valley Twins #41,* **The
Twins Get Caught.**

SWEET VALLEY TWINS™

COULD *YOU* BE THE NEXT SWEET VALLEY READER OF THE MONTH?

ENTER BANTAM BOOKS' SWEET VALLEY CONTEST & SWEEPSTAKES IN ONE!

Calling all Sweet Valley Fans! Here's a chance to appear in a Sweet Valley book!

We know how important Sweet Valley is to you. That's why we've come up with a Sweet Valley celebration offering exciting opportunities to have YOUR thoughts printed in a Sweet Valley book!

"How do I become a Sweet Valley Reader of the Month?"

It's easy. Just write a one-page essay (no more than 150 words, please) telling us a little about yourself, and why you like to read Sweet Valley books. We will pick the best essays and print them along with the winner's photo in the back of upcoming Sweet Valley books. Every month there will be a new Sweet Valley Twins Reader of the Month!

And, there's more!

Just sending in your essay makes you eligible for the Grand Prize drawing for a trip to Los Angeles, California! This once-in-a-life-time trip includes round-trip airfare, accommodations for 5 nights (economy double occupancy), a rental car, and meal allowance. (Approximate retail value: $4,500.)

Don't wait! Write your essay today.
No purchase necessary. See the next page for Official rules.

ENTER BANTAM BOOKS' SWEET VALLEY READER OF THE MONTH SWEEPSTAKES

OFFICIAL RULES:

READER OF THE MONTH ESSAY CONTEST

1. No Purchase Is Necessary. Enter by hand printing your name, address, date of birth and telephone number on a plain 3" x 5" card, and sending this card along with your essay telling us about yourself and why you like to read Sweet Valley books to:

READER OF THE MONTH
SWEET VALLEY TWINS
BANTAM BOOKS
YR MARKETING
666 FIFTH AVENUE
NEW YORK, NEW YORK 10103

2. Reader of the Month Contest Winner. For each month from June 1, 1990 through December 31, 1990, a Sweet Valley Twins Reader of the Month will be chosen from the entries received during that month. The winners will have their essay and photo published in the back of an upcoming Sweet Valley Twins title.

3. Enter as often as you wish, but each essay must be original and each entry must be mailed in a separate envelope bearing sufficient postage. All completed entries must be postmarked and received by Bantam no later than December 31, 1990, in order to be eligible for the Essay Contest and Sweepstakes. Entrants must be between the ages of 6 and 16 years old. Each essay must be no more than 150 words and must be typed double-spaced or neatly printed on one side of an 8 1/2" x 11" page which has the entrant's name, address, date of birth and telephone number at the top. The essays submitted will be judged each month by Bantam's Marketing Department on the basis of originality, creativity, thoughtfulness, and writing ability, and all of Bantam's decisions are final and binding. Essays become the property of Bantam Books and none will be returned. Bantam reserves the right to edit the winning essays for length and readability. Essay Contest winners will be notified by mail within 30 days of being chosen. In the event there are an insufficient number of essays received in any month which meet the minimum standards established by the judges, Bantam reserves the right not to choose a Reader of the Month. Winners have 30 days from the date of Bantam's notice in which to respond, or an alternate Reader of the Month winner will be chosen. Bantam is not responsible for incomplete or lost or misdirected entries.

4. Winners of the Essay Contest and their parents or legal guardians may be required to execute an Affidavit of Eligibility and Promotional Release supplied by Bantam. Entering the Reader of the Month Contest constitutes permission for use of the winner's name, address, likeness and contest submission for publicity and promotional purposes, with no additional compensation.

5. Employees of Bantam Books, Bantam Doubleday Dell Publishing Group, Inc., and their subsidiaries and affiliates, and their immediate family members are not eligible to enter the Essay Contest. The Essay Contest is open to residents of the U.S. and Canada (excluding the province of Quebec), and is void wherever prohibited or restricted by law. All applicable federal, state, and local regulations apply.

READER OF THE MONTH SWEEPSTAKES

6. Sweepstakes Entry. No purchase is necessary. Every entrant in the Sweet Valley High, Sweet Valley Twins and Sweet Valley Kids Essay Contest whose completed entry is received by December 31, 1990 will be entered in the Reader of the Month Sweepstakes. The Grand Prize winner will be selected in a random drawing from all completed entries received on or about February 1, 1991 and will be notified by mail. Bantam's decision is final and binding. Odds of winning are dependent on the number of entries received. The prize is non-transferable and no substitution is allowed. The Grand Prize winner must be accompanied on the trip by a parent or legal guardian. Taxes are the sole responsibility of the prize winner. Trip must be taken within one year of notification and is subject to availability. Travel arrangements will be made for the winner and, once made, no changes will be allowed.

7. 1 Grand Prize. A six day, five night trip for two to Los Angeles, California. Includes round-trip coach airfare, accommodations for 5 nights (economy double occupancy), a rental car -- economy model, and spending allowance for meals. (Approximate retail value: $4,500.)

8. The Grand Prize winner and their parent or legal guardian may be required to execute an Affidavit of Eligibility and Promotional Release supplied by Bantam. Entering the Reader of the Month Sweepstakes constitutes permission for use of the winner's name, address, and the likeness for publicity and promotional purposes, with no additional compensation.

9. Employees of Bantam Books, Bantam Doubleday Dell Publishing Group, Inc., and their subsidiaries and affiliates, and their immediate family members are not eligible to enter this Sweepstakes. The Sweepstakes is open to residents of the U.S. and Canada (excluding the province of Quebec), and is void wherever prohibited or restricted by law. If a Canadian resident, the Grand Prize winner will be required to correctly answer an arithmetical skill-testing question in order to receive the prize. All applicable federal, state, and local regulations apply. The Grand Prize will be awarded in the name of the minor's parent or guardian. Taxes, if any, are the winner's sole responsibility.

10. For the name of the Grand Prize winner and the names of the winners of the Sweet Valley High, Sweet Valley Twins and Sweet Valley Kids Essay Contests, send a stamped, self-addressed envelope entirely separate from your entry to: Bantam Books, Sweet Valley Reader of the Month Winners, Young Readers Marketing, 666 Fifth Avenue, New York, New York 10103. The winners list will be available after April 15, 1991.